GRAY

the story of a guy

Laura Ross

Follow me around:

IG: lmwrites50

CONTENTS

She would ask,
"What do you get from white and black together?"
I don't know is what I say
Something so neutral
The basic color gray
A few opposite shades of hue
A hint of difference to make something new
She an acre and I a degree
Though in the end still personality
Just being nice
And showing some consideration;
Showing love
Inspiring the inspiration
I remember once
When my darling asked me
How they could be so mean
I told her we're mixing Gray
Not the ugly color green.

PROLOGUE

"WHAT DO YOU GET when you mix black and white together?" Sylvia asked me, her blue eyes filled with a curiosity that made me hella uncomfortable. I shrugged, partially as an answer to that random ass question and a conveyance of my actual confusion.

"Hell if I know," I told her because hell, I really didn't. "Why is the sky blue?"

We stood against the brick wall just outside Easton Rogue High and were in the middle of laughing at some geeky-looking kid I vaguely recognized from Spanish class fall to the ground.

It was sort of...unconventional, our relationship. Since meeting in that holy place we made it a point to pick up as many bad habits as possible. At least I did. I made it my mission to expose the sheltered church girl to the ways of the world, so to speak, and one of those ways involved heavy indica and ditching out on those useless classes.

"Oh, crap!" The tiny white girl gasped after choking on the blunt. "Devin look! He's falling."

I barely get the words out before I see the Geeky Kid Kid continue to roll down the grassy hill he fell down. But it ain't exactly a clumsy fall he took, I notice, as the three guys stroll into view seconds after. They're howling by the time Geeky Kid reaches the bare bottom of the patch where a shit ton of mud rests. He's covered in the goo by the time he stands up and shuffles away crying.

It doesn't take a rocket scientist to put two-and-two together and see they pushed the kid.

I bite down on my lip to keep a lid on my do-good sensor. Doing good ain't the point of us skipping school. And it sure ain't the type of morals I was raised with.

Sylvia's giggles at the chubby geek kid's misery and rough chokes on the blunt bring me back from the moral tango my brain danced. Fuck wrong or right, I thought, snatching the blunt from her hands.

"Puff and pass girl," I warn before pulling real hard on the bud. "That's a cardinal rule when in space."

"Space?"

"*Space*," I emphasize with flailed hands to highlight my point. "You know, getting high into the clouds with this joint shit."

"Ohhhhh..." She said before falling into yet, another fit of giggles. Frankly, I was getting real sick of her. "Smoking weed!"

Sylvia continues to babble on about being able to see if the sky really is blue as my mind drifts into the ether. I wonder where that kid went and what the hell his name is. Those dudes who knocked him down the hill like Friday night's trash looked really familiar too, in fact, like I'd smoked with them before. That do-good sensor kicks off in my head even after I finish the blunt. I didn't adore the heaviness in my chest at the reality that we'd stood by and laughed while he got kicked. That he was falling down in misery while we got high in the sky.

Then I hear the cries.

Those same whimpers from before are not loud and ringing in my ears. It's Geeky Kid. The increased volume of his cries let me know he's right beside me now, yet I don't see anyone when I open my eyes to scan the empty schoolyard.

"So you kickin it with snow bunnies now or what?"

The coarse voice jerked me from my thoughts and I blinked hard to focus on the set of three new faces before me.

"What do you guys think happens when black and white mix together?" I hear Sylvia ask innocently to the guys ahead.

They laugh of course.

"Why don't you and Dev answer us that?"

It isn't really a question. More so, it's a dare. A challenge to both she and I, but I can't think straight with all the crying in my ears from the kid I no longer saw.

"Yo Sylvia chill on that black and white shit." I grumble at her.

"Barbie is high as hell!" One of the dudes chortle.

"Wake up and stop being a fake bitch, Devin. Can't you see me talking to you?" The one in the middle demands.

Then the crying stops. And the fog clears enough for me to identify the all black american teens glaring daggers at me.

"Ty?" I ask.

"So now you see me. Smell the coffee and look at me when I talk to you. You murderer."

"Say what?"

"You're there. And I'm here. Because of YOU!"

Ty raises his hand to punch the living shit out of me, and it's a blow I merely don't got the energy to block. That blow, like that stupid do-good meter, was gonna hit me full frontal and without a means to dodge.

Suddenly there's yelling in the background.

Not the background, I realized, but far off into the distance there's a girl pacing backwards from us and calling out to me. It's Sylvia.

"Black and white?!" She screams, her blond hair whipping as carefree in the wind as her continued laughter. "You get gray!"

One

CHANGING PLACES

"*DEVIN! GET YOUR STUPID ass in this kitchen!*" *My mother called to me.*

What a bitch, I thought as I dragged myself into the kitchen— unknowingly entering the battlefield of fried meat and shame. Helen was wearing her usual uniform for the weekends; a scarf with a wool nightgown and a hair wrap. Rocking the Aunt Jemima image. It was the middle of winter, and the middle of school, and the middle of my sophomore experience. My life. My hell. We glared at each other for a moment, and then I grabbed the broom and began sweeping the mess I made on the floor. Since the Cooper family owned no maid I was the keeper around here sometime. Most of the time, however, Yvonne, my sister, would do most of the cleaning while Helen trashed the house bringing in her random boyfriends every damn two weeks. I never complained though. I knew she could easily put me back out on the street like last time when I "bad mouthed" her. Plus, I wouldn't want to upset Yvonne anymore by the name we all feared in this household—the cops. Social workers and visitation rights were definitely a way I wouldn't want to roll, especially with Yvonne being only twelve.

"What the hell did I tell you about being in the kitchen? When you make a mess— you clean it, regardless! Give me the broom, stupid!" I extended the tool out to her where she snatched it, slapped me, and sent me away. Jeez, all I did was spill a little bit of dry Kool-aid. I knew we had ants, but I didn't think the problem to be as severe as that. Whatever.

I grabbed my coat and my dignity and set off to the outside— not wanting to be there when Helen's date came by. I knew where I would go. Planned it out as soon as I woke up this morning:

Trice's house.

Patrice Newbern. My best friend. My rock. I went to her for reasons I couldn't explain. When Helen threw me out for that week, I stayed there. Of course, her parents didn't know I did. Waking up extra early and leaving was a tough one. I rarely did that for school. Yeah, that was dedication. Trice was a five-foot-three, tan skinned girl with a sweet personality and a hot body. She had her quirks—but who doesn't? The thing was, she was a refuge from my mother and very best friend which was a larger than life deal. Me and Trice went as far back as middle school but our relationship as friends halted after I moved away.

I reached her doorstep and rapped on the door, waiting for a Newbern. Trice met me at the door with a sly smile. I mirrored her expression. I leaped inside to a warm atmosphere. This was why I loved this place. Such a homey feeling. Like love or something. Trice's face lit up as she dragged me to the bedroom. Her bedroom. Where the magic took place. Another reason of my love of staying here.

When we reached the bedroom, I went to the bed and she sprang upon me with sheer force. She had been thinking the same thing I had this morning. That was something we always seemed to agree on.

"Shit, wake up!" Trice exclaimed and tossed my pants to me in bed. I woke up sort of groggy and confused and unaware of what was going on.

"How long was I out?" I yawned.

I was routinely putting my clothes back on, while she adjusted herself and ran down the hall and into the bathroom.

She craned her neck around the threshold and whispered fiercely, "My parents are back from work."

I looked at her more alertly now. "*Shit* is right."

I mumbled as I started for the window. I attempted to shimmy down a drain pipe with a misstep and crashed. I fell with my back to the world into the bushes. It was funny, but painful. I sucked it up like a man and stumbled down the street into the misty night.

I contemplated going to school or not when I woke up the next morning. Well, I guess it would've been easier for me to say no, but I couldn't say it because of Yvonne's cries. "Devin, c'mon!" She yelled.

I woke up with a huff and shooed her from my room so I could get dressed for school. She could be so annoying some damn time. It was like she was egging me on. But I can't change her.

"Damn!" I opened the medicine cabinet to discover no trace of toothpaste. Pissed, I ran to Helen's room and pounded on the door. She groaned from sleep so I knocked harder and longer.

"What!" She screamed angrily.

"Ain't no more toothpaste."

"And?" She said defiantly. I bit my lip to keep from tearing the door off its hinges. "What am I supposed to do about it?"

"I don't know- buy some? I'd like to go to school with a little more than the taste of DoubleMint."

"Well, I guess you better handle that yourself. I got my own toothpaste in here."

"Can I use some of yours...ma?" *bitch?* I thought. She really was. "Vonnie and I would really like that."

The door flew open and a lash of pain overcame my cheek; she had slapped me. At that very instant I had to think— would foster care take us away if I were to hit this woman? Just a small blow to the gut? With just enough force to send her rude ass flying through the walls of our house? I refrained and stormed off; first in Yvonne's room to bring her outside, and then to civilization. We stood outside to wait for her bus so we could hurry off to school without my temper flaring or the law getting in the way.

"Devin ...?" Her large, hazel eyes bore into mine. Demanding attention.

"What!" I snapped. I cleared my throat and composed myself. The look on her face made me want to kill myself, but I restated, "What," a little more gently.

"Can I ride with you to school today?" She inquired while eyeing my silver Volkswagen down.

I sighed.

"I missed the bus." she added.

I exhaled sharply, "Well, why didn't you tell me that before?"

She squeezed her purse. "Well, you scared the hell out of me back there when you yelled at Mom like that. I thought you'd go Hulk on me." Huh, I hadn't realized I was yelling.

She started for my car and I yanked her backward. Glaring at her head-on. No guilt. "Listen. If you want a ride from me— you'll have to stop cursing. It's not ladylike and shows that you ain't got no home training. It's not going down like that, you hear?" I preached. There should be no confusion in it all. Yvonne was a young lady now, and she couldn't be carrying herself in such a way. Those were crazy words coming from my lips, but I believed it all though.

The 'young lady' looked me in the eyes and said lightly, "I miss daddy..." I could challenge her femininity no longer with those words.

So all I could really do was nod, start the engine, and say, "I do, too."

When I walked through the doors of Easton Rogue High, I spotted Trice's girlfriends (who were all whores, by the way) and headed toward them with an inquisition, "Where's Patrice?" I grilled them.

The one with the funky, green hair answered, "Somewhere."

"Where 'somewhere'?"

"We don't know!" Retorted the short, skanky girl I believed to be Nora Albert. Nora was one of those fake friends Trice hung out with a lot more since I left DC a few years ago when the accident happened.

That horrible accident.

I sighed in frustration and flipped her off. I remembered Trice telling me something about her. I didn't care to acknowledge it. I glared at them, all three of them, and inquired, "Where the hell is the girl?"

"What's going on?" Said Trice's voice from behind me. I smiled and she said, "Did you just flip Nora off?"

"Yeah, well, she deserved it—" I guided her toward the men's room.

She halted and watched me like I was demented. "What're you doing?"

I eyed her knowingly, and she squinted her eyes— she didn't get it. "I...uh...a quickie? Before class, I mean."

"No."

"Why? *Please*?" I entreated her.

"Devin, nah. This is school. Besides, don't you have exams today?" She asked, knowing the answer before me. I sighed and started down the hall— thinking it useless to beg her any further.

"I'll see you later, bye." I didn't care to hear anymore. It was clear, she wasn't into it. Trice knew all along that I anticipated that moment. Our 'quickie' that we share every morning in different places. Her and her partial ways were frankly pissing me off lately. I wondered what was up with her. She was becoming more and more like her friends each day; the three trampatiers.

Two

The Benefits of Being Broke

I COULD NEVER AFFORD to take my girlfriends out on dates. However, actually admitting it out loud was crushing. Ever since Yvonne and I moved back to Washington DC with Helen three months ago I could never find a decent job. It all came easy living with Quincy— Yvonne's father. I didn't know mine (Helen told me once that he never existed and that I should never question her about him again). Quincy Masters was an okay guy; buying us the things we needed and wanted. He was far from rich once we moved to Queens, but operated with trust and peace and gave me the freedom I needed. Ever since the incident three years ago, the family was chewed up. Quincy kept the family together before that though, and ingrained in me, as the oldest kid in the house of three, that my word was my bond and to trust nobody. I was ten when he told me this, and even though it may not have been the best advice, they became the words I lived for. That was good enough for me.

The story of that chapter in my life was very tender. *Sore.* When Yvonne was born, my mother began cheating on Quincy. Even though that pushed my cool ass stepdad to the edge, it never made him leave— at least not for that. The driving force that propelled him out the door was the incident...

He couldn't take her shit anymore, so they split. Helen stayed here in DC whereas Quincy moved away to Queens, New York. He threatened to sue for sole custody of Yvonne, but instead they made an agreement: Quincy would raise us, but still allow his bitter wife to claim me on her taxes. While he only fought for custody for his biological kids, he took me with him after I begged to. I got involved with some gang drama shortly before I fled to live with him, and that only made living in the city I called home more off limits. Life with Helen before Quincy was cold, but after the incident that coldness was replaced with hatred. She'd beat us for no reason at all with hot skillets, starve us, burn cigarettes in our naturally long hair, and reassure us daily of how much she regretted birthing us. I knew a life there without him would have ended in death (either mine or Helen's), so he let me stay with him. After that though, he was never the same.

Gone was the amiable drug dealer I knew as my only role model since four, and in his place became a distant shell of a person. He smoked for hours each day and sometimes went long stretches without eating. Smoking became his breakfast and breath, his only coffee to jumpstart himself into the hell of the next day. While he was literally the same Quincy, a piece broke in him, and after he died three months ago it broke something in me, too. I guess that was influential enough for me to start. I remember Yvonne asking how it tastes. She was eleven. "It tastes yucky! If you smoke your tongue will change colors and fall off!" I've always urged Yvonne to do what was best- even if it was too late for me. We needed at least one survivor in this family

I was sitting in my first day, since I got my classes switched, of Sex ed. There was nowhere else I could go, no other class I could take. I wasn't uncomfortable talking about these subjects, but I just didn't like to place my sex life in spotlight. Even though it was just life.

Our Sex ed instructor was hot as hell, though. Ms. Christina Sanchez. She had a banging body, nice lips, and a great rack. When she swayed pass me, I could smell her perfume run through my nose— awaken my senses. Lord only knows the dirty scenarios that played through my mind every time I saw her. Walking through the halls with those large, brown, searching eyes. And my damn dreams.

"Where do STD's originate, Devin?" She called on me.

I shrugged and replied, "It's in itself. Sex."

That was a doozy. She nodded and ordered me to stay after class to speak with her. I refused and was set off with a warning (she cussed me out). After class, I met her and she reprimanded with a "gentle" voice this time. I gave her my best smile and she hadn't flinched an inch.

"What is that supposed to implicate?" she asked snootily.

I didn't know what that term meant, but I thought nothing of it and my impatience caught the best of me when I grabbed and kissed her. She was petite and not much of a fight, so I sort of had control of the situation in the first place. When I released her, she pounded my chest and pulled at my hair and scratched me, and screamed. I could take it all except the screaming; so I turned left.

"You're magic, *mami*." I called to her with a sly smile.

She attempted to run after me, but another class came pouring in, and she had been trapped with questions and laughter. Whatever the penalty, I didn't care.

That kiss was worth it.

I lay in bed that same night and think. Since there was nothing I could do, but listen to Helen and her boyfriend fight over nothing. I just chose the safe side. First, I leaned over to crank up the music— the sound of near catastrophe struck me; Helen. They were still ranting and raving over nonsense, and I couldn't handle it. I needed action.

I wanted to do something...but what? It was midnight and everything was closed, and Trice was acting like a royal bitch over the past week. I try and call her, she doesn't answer the damn phone. I try texting, but remembered her losing her phone at the mall last week. There was nothing I could do.

About an hour later, I came to terms and attempted to call her again. Unfortunately, I can't on my cell, because of the glitch in my plan, and now I can make no outgoing calls. I stood and sauntered out of my room and into the hall filled with reverberating screams from downstairs. I pick up the phone and dial Trice's number. I've got to get things right. I thought determinedly.

And then it happened.

When I placed the phone to my ear to listen to the voice I longed to hear, it was replaced by a placid, "phone is now disconnected please consider our great new plans online at..." I stopped it there and threw the phone receiver at the wall.

The crash of it startled my mother and her friend, she screamed, "What the hell was that sound?" I was blinded with fury when I ran down the steps to confront Helen. This was the last straw. No way was I letting her get away with this. I can't even share a call with my fucking girlfriend?

"Helen!" I barked.

"What!" She yelled back at me, surprised.

"What the hell is up with the phone? Why can't I make a call? You didn't pay the bill? Huh?"

The foreign man stepped in front of her and said to me, "Little homey, don't be talking to your mother like that-"

"Little? I don't even know you, and I know that I'm three times the man *you* is, so don't freaking play with me!" The two of us glared at each other.

I was so hot I didn't even feel the tears slip down my cheeks or the sting of the man's blow to the gut. I had been doubled over with the shock of the action. Incognizant to why he'd act on such a notion. I was fighting him in third person. Seeing things blurring in front of me and thinking initially of the law and social workers that would soon be involved in this: Devin punches the ugly dude in the chin, and dodges the oncoming hit that the dude almost inflicts upon him. However,

Helen is smiling and edging away as though the matter was some sort of joke. Devin turns and advances on her.

I don't hit her because she's my mother after all, but I lifted my hand against her and deliberated with my conscience. Why hit her and risk everything? My friends. My girl. Yvonne. There was no way anyone was taking her away from me. Not again.

After all, that little girl was my sanity.

I exhale sharply and storm out the door, leaving Helen alone with her smirk and defeated boyfriend. I head for my car, my old and faithful refuge, and attempt to hop in and go far away or just chill in there and stew. There was only one problem; I left my keys in the house. I let my head fall against the steering wheel, I sighed. I was near to bursting. I was just fed up with Helen. I've only lived with this woman for three months, and already she was driving me insane. I have no idea what any man would see in her. There wasn't even an ounce of love in that cold woman's heart. I mean, she had some sort of heart for taking us in, but the love wasn't there at all. I just hated her. There was no other way to put it. How could any woman- any parent- stand back and watch their child fight an old, ugly dude with halitosis and bad manners was beyond me. I began to open the door to go back into the house, but a miracle came rapping upon my car door. My sanity.

I smiled and unlocked the passenger side to let Yvonne inside. Her eyes were bloodshot and she threw me my car keys. When I saw her face I thought the worst. Did that bastard touch her? Did Helen? If that was the case, then I wouldn't care if the authorities interfered— someone would've been killed.

I clenched my hands upon the grip of the driver's side to exit.

Yvonne caught my arm and sobbed hurriedly, "Please, just drive Devin! I don't want to be here anymore." she continued. "I hate him." She said that last part mostly to herself.

I watched her lock her door and buckle up. She was cradling herself and looking out the window.

"Drive!" she screamed.

I accelerated, and sped down the street— hitting forty in a mere twenty-five speeding zone. I slowed the car when we arrived at the Holy Ghost Church of God.

When I parked the car, I turned to a calmer Yvonne and whispered, "What did he do to you, Vonnie?" I swallowed and prepared for the worst.

She turned to me and said, "You're almost out of gas." She reached into her pocket and gave me a fifty dollar bill. My eyes widened at the sight of it and she explained, "I snatched it from Mom's boyfriend when he wasn't looking yesterday. I had planned to run away with that money, but I forgot about it and put it away. Until now— what I just saw between you and Mom ...that was unforgiving. I don't know what happened with you guys, but whatever the reason, Mom's reaction was what drove me to, more than ever, decide to get away." she peered out into the darkness at the church we stopped in front of. She turned to me and said questioningly, "There's someone waving us away, Dev."

All I could do was look at her with awe. I paid no attention to whoever it was waving us away or forward, it didn't matter to me. All I cared for was Yvonne— my little Vonnie. Who could pollute an innocent soul like hers to the point of loathe? I know if I ever reached that point, I probably would beat myself up about it.

"Vonnie...first of all...why did you steal from him? I mean, I 'm with you all the way about not liking him, but I don't want you taking anything from anybody unless you have the means to pay him or her back— do you understand me?"

I looked at the little girl authoritatively, and she turned away with defiance. I tapped her shoulder lightly, but displaying dominance. She whipped her head around and watched me with her eyes full of tears. She was such a crybaby.

"Yvonne, what the hell are you crying for? I'm just trying to tell you not to be doing bad things. But you apparently don't like to listen to me. I don't want you making the same mistakes I have."

"All right. I won't. But—"

"The dude waving us down? I got it, hold on a minute." I unlocked my door and exited the car without further ado. I would finally see who it was waving us away. The nerve of some people, I thought.

"Hello young man. How are you this morning?"

I looked around and realized that the sun was rising and I had to get that little girl home before her bedtime— as created by myself. Her curfew. I nodded in response to the man who had exited the church, and he watched me with large, blue eyes.

"So," I began, trying to make friendly conversation. Especially since I was treading on his land. "I guess I better leave or you'll call the cops on me, huh?"

I turned and started for my car, but was halted with his wide, flat hand on my shoulder. It stopped me all right.

"Wait a minute, son." He started. "This is a church of God— and all persons are welcome."

"Then why were you waving us away?"

"I wanted for you to come on in— to talk." He paused. "And what do you mean when you say, 'we'?" He asked me.

He fooled me. It looked as though he actually cared for me. Us. What I thought. I could not deny the sense of...joy? Pride? Acceptance? I had no idea what it was, and I was more than willing not to find out. It shouldn't bother me— what other people thought of me. That I was an abomination in the eyes of the Lord, as quoted from Helen. She also said that about Yvonne, too, but I shied from the thought. She was the last person in hell who I'd rather think about, without wanting to choke something within reach. But I didn't like thinking thoughts like that in front of the very guy I was an "abomination" of.

"Oh yeah." I said. I forgot to mention her. I didn't want to be a pest by telling him I had a crew with me. "Her?"

"Your girlfriend?" He assumed.

I burst into a comfortable laughter. I actually enjoyed laughing around this place.

"No." I uttered. "Far from it. That's my little sister."

He nodded with a grin. "Well, what's the little bugger's name?"

"Yvonne." *Bugger?* No. My sanity. She really was.

"Well," he said. "I'm Pastor Timothy Blake. Most refer to me as Pastor Tim, though— I'd love it if you could become one of those most." Pastor Tim had the weirdest smile on his face.

White people, I started to say, but refrained. Not allowing the Helen Cooper side of myself to be shown. All too aware of her prejudices against ninety-nine percent of the world population. Partial to the world and narcissistic to the one percent— herself.

I had been drowned in deliberation to notice Yvonne speaking with Pastor Tim about whatever they were discussing at the moment.

I frowned at her. "I didn't tell you to leave the car, Vonnie."

I scolded her tenuously. Pastor Tim watched me in amazement. "It's either you're very protective or just a meanie. I was just talking to the girl."

He sounded truly offended. That only added to the guilt of me feeling like a bad brother.

I bowed my head in shame.

"My bad. It's just— I don't like her being out of my sight when we're in town. It makes me nervous." I admitted.

There was no shame in that. I liked protecting my sister— that wasn't a sin.

Was it? I had no prior biblical schooling. Thanks to both of our parents.

Pastor Tim nodded and escorted us into the chapel. As soon as I walked in— and I mean the exact second— I felt this relief wash over me. Like I could do anything. Liberated...as though anything was possible. I sighed to myself, wishing that was true. If so, then I would've had my own apartment by now. Away from Helen Cooper and her bull...I didn't want cuss while in the "eyes of the Lord".

"So, what brings you two young souls here three in the morning?" he inquired.

I shrugged. He had led us to the kitchen of the church, where something good was cooking. My stomach churned. I saw Yvonne flinch as well.

"Well, my car ran out of gas..." I turned away; avoiding him and the vending machine was a tough one. I tried not to think of that money Yvonne showed me earlier. I felt as if I had done something blasphemous.

I would willingly take the blame if I had to, though. She was only a kid after all.

"Devin? I think little Yvonne had told me your name was, will you care to join me in my late night feasting? I'm asking if little Yvonne can come along, too. Would that be all right...Mr. Protector?"

I watched the Pastor, skeptical of his words. That was too idyllic.

"What's in it for you?" I asked him suspiciously– narrowing my eyes.

He beamed, I had no idea why he was this happy, but it was kind of irritating. Grilling time. "Why are you here this time of night? Morning?" I asked.

"Why are you here this morning?" He countered.

"Touché." I grumbled and sat at one of the booths in the dining area, Yvonne joined me.

"Well," he began. "There are certain conditions. I would like it if you could join us for church this Sunday. Both of you. It would be excellent if you guys could bring the family. How 'bout it?"

I sat to contemplate, while Yvonne spouted, "Sure! I'm hungry!" I wanted to lean over and slap the living stars out of that girl, but I thought instead. That offer didn't sound too bad, but I wouldn't want to seem as eager for food as Yvonne had. I could've stopped by McDonald's or something on the way home. Food was no obstacle.

"I guess I can come for the Word— sounds worth it." I shrugged and he guided Yvonne into the kitchen to help prepare and serve the food.

I hadn't eaten dinner, and it sounded like a good proposition. When the Pastor came back with our food and my sister he asked me something that seemed like a dream.

"Devin, you guys seem sort of tired. I wouldn't mind it if the two of you stayed the...morning I guess...here. How 'bout it?"

Again with the persuasive "how 'bout it?" technique. I sorted through my options and there were none I could think of. So I accepted. He said that there were boarding rooms upstairs— he said he used it for storage, but was willing to clean and dust it a little before we went for bed. Everything seemed too good to be true. I didn't want to ruin anything, so I just nodded and allowed him to lead the two of us up the stairs. He asked if I needed to call a parent.

"No." I said. Mostly because it was true. Helen shared no interest in knowing her childrens' where being, so I decided it the best thing for Vonnie.

The moment I walked in— and I mean the exact second— I felt this relief wash over me. Like I could do anything. Liberated...as though anything was possible.

And with that, I grew my wings and began to fly.

Three

TALKING JAPANESE WHILE EATING PIZZA

PASTOR TIM HAD TAKEN us to school in the morning, and filled my gas tank to an all time high. I knew all his deeds were meant for some sort of exchange, so I focused on getting a job. Whatever money I'd make, I'd save it towards my apartment, pay back what Pastor Tim welcomes us to, and give whatever is left to Yvonne as allowance. But I shouldn't be thinking like that, though. I had to remember to get a job first.

And I knew where to start.

When school ended, I headed to this pizza joint that was now hiring sixteen-year olds under strict conditions and desperation. Desperate because of the high levels of resignation, and low tolerance. I was surprised at how anyone could possibly be fired from an easy job such as this. I held my success in the highest esteem; pizza— my favorite subject.

The boss, Donna Leanly, was a cute, middle aged woman with a funky attitude and a pistol— meaning she was one of those fine soccer moms with bite. I wasn't ashamed of that. She was a very short Jamaican lady– about five foot one— with large, brown eyes, and a beautiful smile. I had found out that she was twenty-nine and happily married from the cook. Tyrone Zelman, a seventeen-year old bad ass without a sunny future and branded by two kids and another on the way. We went to the same school , and in all the years I've known Tyrone, he's always been known to flirt; suffering from a terminal case of, "the eye" as some may call it, but I had always referred to it as "flirting". He was forced to get a job, because of his immediate view of mundane authority— in other words, Tyrone was a self absorbed slacker with a driving motivation of his kids. Donna was his sister-in-law and the two acted as though they've known each other their entire lives. Splashing each other with condiments, and the affectionate "swearing" at each other.

"You got the job." she had said to me coldly

I thanked her and told her I would start the next day at three o' clock. She rolled her eyes and drifted. I felt like dancing. If there were any other words to describe my happiness— then that was how I had felt.

Tyrone sauntered over to me with a hard expression on his face, and nodded a greeting. I signaled my response back.

"How you been?" I asked him nonchalantly. I had to be cool. He eyed me down and chuckled to himself.

Tyrone shook his head and replied, "Kids been actin' bad as hell."

I eyed him down curiously. What was he trying to tell me? Did he think I'd relate to him somehow? If Tyrone had that sort of mindset , then he was one hundred percent wrong! Why must everyone confide their issues to me?

"So," I said to him, "I like the, uh, new job." My eyes were now scanning the place— feigning amazement. "A real kicker." What a lie that was, and I knew he would see

though it.

"Man, shut your ass up." He said defensively.

I smiled. It was amusing to piss him off. Tyrone chuckled deeply and said, "Main reason I work here is so that I could get free pizza. Seriously, they be leavin' a whole lotta' leftovers at the end of the day. I can hook you up if you start tonight."

"What do you mean when you say, 'hook up'?"

"You know?" he insisted lowly.

"You be askin' Donna don't you? Man get outta' here with that!" I pointed out.

"Who said I asked?" Tyrone watched me with a steadfast smirk that meant business. "You know what I'm saying?"

I knew what he was saying, but couldn't quite grasp the purpose. Why would someone steal leftover pizzas? Especially when you were related to the boss? Crazy.

I decided to mentally branch away from the subject. "You 'bout to go, homey?"

"Yeah. I gotta' go see somebody." I groaned.

"I know where you goin'?" Tyrone taunted.

"I bet you do." I said coolly.

"That girl of yours? What's her name? Patty? Pam? Panorama?"

I watched him skeptically. "You kiddin' right? I guess you won't know."

"Whatever. Listen, I got some smokes— you care to join me outside?" he asked, being a sarcastic douche. I accepted and followed Tyrone out the door. After all, I hadn't had a cig in like twenty years, it felt like.

***

"Yo, man you stupid!" Tyrone exclaimed.

I had just told him of the time, when I lived in New York, I was about to sleep with this girl who was hideous and had the clap. Well, it was believed that she had, but I was drunk and foolish that night, and didn't feel the need to place my health on the line. What Tyrone had been tripping about was the reality of Yvonne walking in on me, screaming, and running off. I ultimately escaped by chasing the ten-year old down the block.

"She woke up every neighbor with those damn, frantic ass, whale calls." I ended.

Tyrone was hunched over with laughter; didn't know what to do with himself. When the laughter had subsided I asked him how his girl was doing.

"Sasha— man, she cool. All she do is nag my ass, man! I swear I just put up with her for the boy's sake. As long as she act right around my kids then I'm straight. Man, having kids can change a person."

I nodded. And for a long time, there was a lingering awkwardness in the atmosphere until the calls from Donna pierced the air. We jumped.

"I better go." I said. We exchanged a pound and departed. It was as simple as that.

I went to my car, got in it, started the engine, and sped away to the Royal Bitch's palace.

I approached the doorstep to greet, yet again, another Newbern when the wooden door swung open before my fist could greet it. I knew her parents weren't home so I looked up and mumbled,

"Trice, what— what the hell?" I roared.

There was a tall, tan, white dude in the doorway who was eyeing me down with a frown. I shoved him away; further inside the house.

"What you doin' with my girl, dog? Son of a b-"

"Hey!" a soprano voice screamed from the threshold of the living room. It was Trice. The bitch.

"Devin!" her face shifted from frustration to disbelief. Trice leaped to the doorway and cooed the white dude and sent him on his way. She ordered me to get inside the house before she called the cops- and I reluctantly obliged. The authority was a fear of mine. She shut the door and said, "Devin sit down I want to—"

"Hell no! We stay right here. Now tell me who that was?" I hollered.

"Devin, no! Sit DOWN!" She ranted. "This isn't good for me." She murmured.

I massaged my temples and glowered at her. Hate circulating through my being. Pure hate. And I was an expert at how to hate because of Helen's doing.

I turned on my heel and jetted to my car. I heard her sobbing and wanted nothing more than to gather her in my arms and calm her down. But deep down, even though we were never really official I knew we were no more. Now I just had to convince myself that. I was in my car when I heard Trice wailing and crying for me to go back, and a rap song on the radio about a bank. Trice's screams overpowered the music so I roared the engine, flipped her off, and blasted the music until I could hear my thoughts no more.

Four

FAR OFF

There was no way I could sleep that damn pain off!

Five

A CRY FOR ATTENTION DEFICIT

FATHER TIME RAN PAST me in a blur of colors and heartbreak, that I hadn't even noticed that it was Sunday— the day I vowed to arrive at Holy Ghost Church. My alarm went off at ten a.m., and I rolled out of bed with exhausted determination and a bad attitude. Goodness, I did not feel like doing it. Not after what just happened witch Trice. Not ever.

I was now knocking on Yvonne's bedroom door; she answered with a weary expression and a yawn.

"What?" she asked me, and then yawned again. She looked beat. Eyes and cheeks blotchy and red from slumber and irritation for being awakened. "What is it, Devin?" She said again.

I stretched my body out and replied, "Nothing major. Remember that promise we made to the Pastor for letting us stay the night?"

"Yeah." She nodded and turned and murmured, "I think I have something to wear." I changed my direction to head downstairs and eat some breakfast, but I had faced a problem when I reached the first floor. Something that no child wanted to see at any age and at any time. Oh, Jesus, it was gruesome.

The nasty picture of Helen on the living room c ouch...au naturel; naked. I gasped and yelped, "What the— Helen go upstairs with that, yo! Nobody wants to see that!" I dashed into the kitchen with a traumatized brain and...apprehension. I tried to concentrate on pouring my cereal, but I couldn't control my hands from shuddering. I was truly disgusted by that. Seeing Helen lying there like that...with her tousled hair and wrinkled belly from four c-sections. I had to breathe slowly, in and out, to catch my breath. Yvonne shuffled inside with her pearly whites and pink floral dress. Her hair was brushed to the top of her head and into a neat ponytail; she was also rocking her weekend jewelry: four multicolored bracelets, a light pink necklace and red, studded earrings.

I frowned and walked closer to her, "Take that mess off. You'll look cheap by wearing those things to a formal gathering."

I extended my palm expectantly. She huffed and undressed herself from the excessive accessories, and I put them in my pocket. I was wearing one of Quincy's old suits he could never fit and always wanted to get into. It was an average suit with all the trimmings and quirks; freshly tailored, but a grim, brown color. Brown was the color of sadness, and that was the last thing I needed in my life.

And then it hit me. "Vonnie...did you see mama out there?"

She whipped her head around and glared at me; I guess she was still upset with me for taking her jewelry. "Yeah. What about her?"

"She...what was she...wearing?" I asked in a whisper.

She looked suspicious now, "A robe...why?" I shook my head and headed out into the living room with my eyes closed; careful to avoid any unfortunate events. I climbed the stairs and went to my room to change into the sad suit.

Helen was such a monster.

"I want to thank you guys for coming— I really am glad you're here." Pastor Tim said to me when service began.

His blue eyes flashed with fondness and walked into the building. I shrugged and followed him inside with Yvonne hand-in-hand. When we walked inside the sanctuary, I felt as though we were violating or something. It just didn't feel like I was in this safe place where no one could hurt me; it seemed as though we were the invaders to come and disturb the peace. I didn't know, it was just a notion. Yvonne saw one of her friends from school and joined her. I stood there and waved at her with an uneasy face. I wanted her in my sight. But this was a safe place, I had to remind myself that. The liberation had vanished. I felt trapped again. I sighed and wandered off; eventually wandering into the bathroom. I ran the sink water, cupped my hands to catch the water, and threw it on my face. I swiveled the paper towel from its base and wiped my face clean. I needed to clear my head. I looked into the large mirror and scoffed. Boy, did I need my hair braided. I yanked the ponytail holder from my hair and shook my head. What an afro! My curly mane, when wet, reached my armpits. I was told many times before that I had many of my "momma's qualities", but I cringed and hoped he or she was joshing. I wished I had some of my Father's features almost all the time— prayed to know who he was. What he looked like. Did he have a mane like mine? Do I favor him at all? What was his name? Was he still alive today? If he was, then where was he? DC? These were all questions I knew I'd never receive an answer to.

As I strode from the bathroom, hair back in its original, low ponytail, I was dazed and automatically tired again. It was as if I had just awakened and was currently experiencing a groggy feeling. I shrugged it off, and walked through the doors of the sanctuary. I guess it was all the thinking I was doing to make myself so lightheaded, I thought.

I had made a double take when I saw how packed the place was. I squinted my eyes in search of a vacant seat. There weren't any. Where would I sit? This was impossible. I go to the bathroom for few seconds and then this. Jeez! I sighed. Where would I sit? There was no way I was sitting with Yvonne and her gang of roses. I looked up, defeated, and saw Pastor Tim waving for my attention in the stands up by the Pastoral chairs— thank God church hadn't started yet. Otherwise, I would've looked like an ass without a face. Going haywire.

I paced to where the reserved seats and sat between the Pastor and a blonde with a black dress. She looked around my age with a round face and a certain cuteness that showed that she was a little sheltered. Pastor Tim had introduced me to the group of people who sat in the cluster near the podium.

I blocked him out until he got to the innocent girl beside me. "...and this is Sylvia Blake. My little girl."

Pastor Tim pinched her cheeks, and she frowned, smacked his hand away, and turned to smile at me. She seemed to make a double take as I had when I walked in here. Her eyes bulged for a moment and then she seemed to mentally compose herself. Sylvia swallowed hard and looked down, her cheeks were flushed. I chuckled under my breath and opened up one of the bibles while we all waited for church to start. What an innocent girl.

When church ended, many people were shaking hands and greeting each other as if they've know them forever. I shook hands as well, just to be polite. I started for the door, but was halted by a small hand on my shoulder. It couldn't have been Yvonne because she could never reach my shoulder. So I whipped around in curiosity and spotted Sylvia Blake smiling with her hot, flushed cheeks and a white rose in her hand.

She extended it and giggled. "I'm sorry about that earlier. My dad still thinks I'm a kid."

I watched her in amazement. She had guts.

"Yeah, well, at least you have one." I said." What's this for?" I turned the rose over and over in my hand. Trying to grasp the purpose she gave it to me.

"Well. It's a peace offering. You know what a white rose symbolizes, right? Friendship. I would love it if you—"

"No thanks kid." I interrupted her and turned to find Yvonne. Where was that little girl? Ugh, now I needed to go on a goose chase.

"Looking for someone?" Sylvia's small voice chimed. Her hands were on Yvonne's shoulders.

Yvonne said, "She's a real, nice lady. I got lost and..."

"I am so glad you're okay!" I breathed. "I was beginning to panic." I hugged her and shooed away and to the car. She smiled and obeyed like always. "Thank you for that, uh, Sylvia. I really have to go, though. Thank you!" I nodded and jogged to the parking lot.

"Wait!" Sylvia called.

I looked up at her from a distance.

She was yelling, "Meet me here tomorrow afternoon! I want to give you something!" I nodded and started the engine. We were riding down the road while I had been thinking, there's no way.

* * *

When I pulled up in the driveway, my eyes bulged when I saw who left the house.

I could've sworn I was tripping, but the person walked up to my car window and spoke with me. I urged Yvonne to go into the house. I jumped out of the car and slammed the door with force.

"Trice! Do not make me cuss when I just got back from church. Please." I said plainly. It was obvious that she'd been crying. I exhaled sharply and said, "Did you speak with Helen? Why did you come here?"

"I came to see you, Dev."

"Don't you dare call me 'Dev'!" I sighed. "Leave, Patrice."

"Devin, you know you don't call me that! I gotta' tell you—"

"Get the hell outta' here!" I hollered from the top of my lungs to the very bottom of my being. I didn't need this. I shoved passed her and stormed into the house.

"Devin—"

I slammed the door to her screams and flew up the stairs and into my room. I could hear Patrice from all the in my room. I opened my bedroom window and bellowed, "If you don't leave then...Patrice just get off my fucking property!"

She sobbed, "Stop calling me that! Devin!"

"Go!" I barked.

She sniffed, watched me with sad eyes, and ran down the street. I assumed she was going to her place, but I didn't care anymore. I was done with it.

As if things could get any worse, I heard a small voice screaming throughout the house. Who was...Yvonne? Was that her screaming like that? I dashed inside her room but discovered that she wasn't there.

"Vonnie!" I roared. I heard her screaming some more from inside the bathroom. I banged on the door.

"Devin stay out! Get mommy!"

"Is something wrong?" I asked.

"...No. Get her, now!" She ordered.

"Vonnie...please...please...tell me what the problem is?" I was almost in tears.

I didn't want anything happening to her. I sat on the floor in front of the bathroom and buried my head in my hands. I felt like dying; Vonnie was in trouble and I didn't know what to do. With Patrice acting this way and Yvonne going crazy and Helen being her normal, spiteful self— I didn't know if I could do it anymore. The bathroom door opened and Yvonne, crying, had blubbered. "Devin...please...take me to the hospital!"

No more had to be said; I knew where I was going next.

Six

ROTTEN TO THE CORE

THE DOCTOR WAS A woman, thank goodness, with a tall stature and experience. I was basically kicked out of the examination room and had to sit in the waiting room. My heart was pounding, and it felt as if my blood were running cold. I couldn't handle it...what if something was wrong with her? What if it required surgery? Could it be fatal? Maybe I was going crazy...maybe the sky was falling down. I wasn't sure, but I was certain of this: if I didn't calm down I'd have an anxiety attack. Maybe I was in the middle of one; it was hard to put into words.

Meanwhile, I scrutinized the door, eager to meet my baby sister with a smile and a sigh of relief. I had to convince myself that she was in a safe place now.

It was very quiet in the waiting room, there were very few people as well. I scanned the room and sighed in exhaustion. This was way too much, all of this stress I was being put under was...unfair. What did I ever do to deserve a punishment like that? Yvonne was my life...if something was wrong with her then I'd...

"Devin Cooper?" a calm voice called out to me. It was the doctor. Beside her was my smiling sister. I grinned ...she was okay.

"Devin, may I speak with you in private?"

"Yeah. Sure." We walked a few paces away from Yvonne.

The doctor shook my hand and said, "Yvonne is perfectly healthy; she's just started her cycle. Do you know about those? It's when a lady..."

"Thank you for that, but I should take off-" I held my hand up to signal that I didn't want to carry the conversation on.

I swallowed hard and ran a hand through my mane of hair. Well...I had no words for this situation. I felt so stupid— why didn't I pick up on it? I knew all about when girls......when ladies...uh...I didn't want to get into it. I just felt like a major asshole. I turned to look at Yvonne, she looked up at me, and turned away. I couldn't see her the same as always, she was a woman now.

"Listen, I already gave her some starter menstruation pads, they're super absorbent—"

"Thank you lady— I will take note of that! Come on Vonnie." I grabbed her by her arm and pulled her to the exit.

When we reached the car, I turned to Yvonne and asked her, "Are you...are you scared?"

"No." She looked at me with gentle eyes and whispered, "But I don't want to talk about it, though."

I backed off and we both got in the car. I started the engine and drove away from the hospital. There were just no words for that.

"Go in the house." I told Yvonne once we reached home. She acquiesced and trudged along. I had the worst feeling in my gut. Like something bad would happen if I were to...no. There was no way I was thinking in the negative. My mind was focused on too much of that.

I eventually got out of the car, sauntered into the house with my eyes closed, and climbed in bed. Feeling traumatized from too many things.

Seven

PAINTING THE TOWN RED

WHEN I WALKED THROUGH the school building the next day, I was initially showered with glares, then it escalated into whispers and incredulous expressions. I shrugged; I was never paranoid, so I kept my stride and allowed the pieces to fall where they may. After all, the last thing I wanted to do was set bad news in haste. I went into homeroom and collapsed at my desk, laying my head against the cold surface. I came a little early, so there were only about three or four people in the classroom. Including the teacher, Mr. Ferguson who was a sadist, bent on self-destruction through bad grades. He had four tufts of hair encircling his scalp, and was a wiz at history, but taught chemistry. I guess he loved being the variable in the equation.

"Wake your white ass up, man. This ain't the Waffle House."

I sat up quickly with a snort of restlessness, and glared at him. Tyrone. I forced a sneer, but knew it looked like I was retarded, so I asked, "Why I gotta' be white? I come from Indian descent."

Tyrone watched me as if I were the dumbest man alive. He frowned when he said, "Yeah, well, with all that hair— you might as well be." He paused and said, "Yo, man, you need that braided or something? I can hook you up."

"Hell nah." I said. Knowing who he'd persist upon.

"Let me finish, dog. Cop this, Juanita do some good hair, man. I can hook you up so that you ain't got to pay."

"Not Juanita..." I groaned. Juanita Rojas was a chubby black girl with bad grammar and too much free time. I remember the first time I allowed her to braid my hair, she tugged so tight I thought she pulled up a tonsil. I didn't let her get to the third row when I ripped away and took my money back. That was the only day I cried since I was able to walk. I hadn't wept even at Quincy's funeral— and that was such a sad day.

"Yo...I need to think about that. I ain't seen that girl in like a month; I don't think she'd even want to braid my hair." I cringed away from the subject and said, "Damn. You know something that's just fazing me? You made it to school, yo. You never come anymore."

He watched me with a calm expression and sighed, "She's pregnant man. I ain't got no time for school when I'm supposed to be taking care of her. I just worry about her now...she ain't got nobody at home to watch over her during the day. So I got to pick the kids up from school and watch them most of the time. She getting' real close to her due date— sometime this month. Lucky I came today at all."

I nodded as I always did when Tyrone gave one of his little *Mein Kempf* speeches. I respected what he did for his family and the sacrifices he made— but they weren't any of my business. So I always shied away from that area.

Class ended, and I went to my locker to grab some things, closed it, and was on my way to Sex ed. I actually had that class for my fourth period— not second. I wanted to see if Ms. Sanchez was in today, so I could... speak with her. Man she was hot, and I wanted nothing more than to—

"Hello, Mr. Cooper." Interjected Ms. Sanchez's placid voice; she seemed to not mind the fact that I planted one on her the week before. "Come with me."

I was about to suggest the same thing. I followed her to her classroom where she ordered me to sit in one of the desks. I resisted and paced toward the door; I shut it. Now we could get down to business. Since it was her free period, then I was off the hook for about thirty minutes. Her eyes were wide, but her face revealed composure. I wondered what bit her. She came closer to me, I smiled, she leaned in toward my face. Then she kissed me. My Sexual Education teacher kissed me, Devin Cooper back and I wasn't quite sure what to make of it. I held her by the shoulders to push away gently to say, "I actually came to get some advice." I continued. "What did you think I came for?"

I was toying with her mind. I stood there and watched her face change colors: from bright pink to a blood red. She was embarrassed. Dear Lord...He only knew how much I wanted to laugh out loud at that moment. I didn't really need advice, I just wanted to come and see what she would do. Frankly, this was the last thing I expected. She yanked herself away from me and walked stiffly to her desk. I came and stood in front of her.

She looked up. "What is it, honey?" her voice was strained.

I grinned, "Never mind, I see you're very much in paperwork so I guess I can come by later...for fourth period."

"N-No. You can tell me now, I'm cool." she insisted. I smiled and thought this good to say and said it: "I was thinking about switching one of my classes. This one. Should I do that or..."

"No! That would be a bad idea. You need this class to graduate, you know?"

"No, you don't. I looked it up, and asked the counselor even. I guess I'll think about staying here, though. It couldn't kill me."

And with that, I turned for the door and exited coolly. That was empowering. Shoved my pride to heights I thought it could never reach; having the hottest teacher in school on the strings you pull was priceless.

As I headed down the hall, I passed more stares and, eventually, Patrice. She was crying and I shooed her away, but she followed me. I got to my locker when I finally exploded.

"What! What the fuck, man? What do you want to tell me?"

I made a scene, she cried harder, threw me a note, and ran away. I shoved it in my pocket and decided to have my own little early release. I crept to my car and started the engine once I was safe and sound and inside. I drove down Memory Lane, passed Heartbreak Hotel, and made a turn on Highland Avenue, where I pulled into the Holy Ghost church parking lot. I got out of the car, realized it was two-thirty, and sat on the side wall of the holy place until three o' clock came. I intended to do nothing and go to a safe place. Here.

* * *

Three o' clock came and went, and before I knew it the clock struck four. I prepared myself to go when I dropped my keys in the grass and stumbled over to retrieve them; it was hard to find keys with camouflage key chains attached to them. It was Yvonne's idea. I remembered the cigarette I had left from a few days ago, took it out on my way to the car and nearly choked from the voice I heard from behind me.

"Jeez— you scared me girl! I damn near...oh, my bad. I didn't mean to curse around you."

Sylvia giggled and practically floated over to me, when she reached me she frowned, took my cig, threw it to the ground, and stomped on it. I had half a mind to slap the living shit out of her, but was afraid of what the Pastor would think.

We were now silent when she said, "You should quit. It's a nasty habit. May I join you?"

"What?" I inquired. She glided over to the passenger side of my car and got in.

"I'll take that as a yes." she called from inside.

I shook my head in disbelief and got in the driver's side. I turned to her and said, "You told me to meet you here today. Didn't you?"

She nodded.

"For what?"

She began, "Reasons. I guess I just felt like talking to you in confidence. So what's up?"

"Listen, kid—"

"Yeah, let's get this straight— I'm fifteen. I'm not a kid."

"You're three years older than my little sister."

"Well, you're four."

"How did you know that?"

"My dad told me a lot."

"Listen, I have no time to play around with little—"

"You better not call me a—"

"Kid?" I challenged. Her face reddened.

"Well, would a kid do this?" she yanked my hair back toward her so our faces met, and kissed me.

It was a very passionate kiss. A kiss too old for a fifteen-year old to know about. If I hadn't known any better, I'd think she was about eighteen kissing like that.

She parted her lips from my greedy ones, and I panted, "Only a very feisty one." I gazed at her, "Church girl gone bad."

"Thank you." She continued. "Where're you headed?"

I swallowed and said, "Home. To Yvonne, I don't like her being there without me."

I said this without a smile because of its trueness. I really didn't like that.

Sylvia's face contorted for a second then she snapped her fingers and exclaimed, "Your sister? Yeah, that's right, my dad told me. Why are you so overprotective over her anyways?"

I turned to glare and blurted, "Shut the hell— I mean."

I had to calm down over a sore spot such as that. She was making me want to talk about the incident. I hadn't told anyone this story...only Helen, Quincy, Trice and I knew this secret. Yvonne was so traumatized she said she didn't remember any of it. Quincy took it to the grave, and that's what I intended to do, too. I did a few breathing exercises, and eventually composed.

"Stay out of my business, all right? She's my baby sister, that's why."

Sylvia placed a hand on my shoulder and said sympathetically, "You can tell me. I don't know if I can relate, because of my being an only child, but maybe I can help you overcome it—"

"I didn't invite you to shrink my damn head, all right?" My temper was unbridled by then.

I wanted to cry when I thought of that accident—what a sore spot. I looked out the window and started, "Yvonne was once a twin. See, when she was about eight or nine, she and her twin, Michael were kidnapped. See, school had let out and they ran off...the teacher said she thought they were still in the building, but then she really couldn't find them and then the cops got involved, and we were separated from my mother to live with Quincy, the twins' father. See, they split after the accident happened."

"Well, what happened to Michael?" Sylvia asked with tears in her eyes. "Please tell me he's at home with Yvonne, too?"

I shook my head and mumbled, "Michael and Yvonne were found a mile away from the pre-school with a man they were looking for for a few years. He had been known to do things like that. Yvonne was found beaten and in a closet...Michael...was found beaten to death, and in a bathtub filled with kerosene to the top. I was young, but remembered everything that happened that day. Yvonne just blanked, and Mikey was a...I gotta' get home now. It's getting late." I cut myself off.

Sylvia was drowning in her own tears by then, I was afraid to look her in the eyes— afraid of what I might do if I were to do that. "If you need anyone to talk to... remember—I'll always be here if you need me, okay?"

"See you later." I concluded.

"Meet me here tomorrow...please? I want to talk to you some more."

I nodded, thinking to myself, maybe I might.

When I walked through the doors of the Cooper residence, I felt like an idiot. Why did I tell her that? Was I on some sort of drug? Maybe I was hanging around Tyrone too long for me to reveal things about my past to anyone. I didn't want to seem soft living on these streets. But me talking about Mikey to anyone at all...k ind of felt good. It really felt like I was getting it off my chest for so long. I trudged up the stairs with a smile, unaware of the tears that slipped down my cheeks. They were actually tears of contentment, something was leaking out of my system.

I knocked on Yvonne's door and said, "You okay in there? You sleep?"

I heard sobs and sniffles and mumbles. I frowned and wiped my face from the tears of joy. "Yvonne are you sick? Where's Helen?"

The sobs were now cries, I pressed my face against the door to listen when I heard, "Shut up...bitch...fucking...kill you."

I fumbled with the locked doorknob, until it swung open to reveal Yvonne crying and laying on the bed... with the same ugly dude from that night hovering over top of her. She was screaming, "Devin! Help me! Oh my gosh..."

"You sonofabitchI'mgonna'fuckingkillyouyoustupidugly—" I was hitting him without knowing it.

I heard Yvonne screaming to the very top of her lungs saying, "Devin stop you're gonna' kill him!"

I wish she had known that that was my very intention. I felt blood splashing my knuckles, and heard the groans of pain, and the protests for life. I paid them no mind while I was doing what I was doing.

"Mommy!" I heard Yvonne yell in fear.

I didn't stop hitting him. Punch after punch, blow after blow— I wanted him dead. My right hand on the bible...this man was going to die tonight. Abruptly, there was a pain that sliced through my arm and I went flying backward. I was screaming and ranting and yelling and Yvonne had been by my side and cooing and screaming for someone to call for nine-one-one. I was bleeding nonstop. My vision was beginning to get hazy when I turned toward the culprit and put the pieces together: one plus one equals two. D-I-E was how to spell die. My name was Devin, and—

Helen was standing at the threshold with a gun.

'Mommy' just shot me.

Eight

Taking a Shower

I NEVER ACTUALLY READ the note that Patrice had given to me the other day. I was lying on the hospital bed with an injured arm and curiosity. Being confined to a bed can really change someone. It was changing me for the worse, though. Mostly because, I had to sit down and think of all the wrong I had caused or had been stuck in. I had every intention of thinking of the wrong, but the good was an iffy. So I thought of the times when I was...happy. Living with Quincy I was content. Never any major conflicts, never any law interventions. The three of us lived in peace for a little while after we fled. I had a few on and off again relationships back in Queens, most were ineffectual (except for this chick I banged at Queens Heights High, named Reina. She was a fiery little Latina who I had fun with for a while as her side until her boyfriend threatened to leave her. She got all guilty after that and ended things). None ever really struck a chord with me the way Patrice had. She started out as my best friend in the world in fifth grade, but something unspoken changed after I left town. I always wondered what happened to her after that, and I still felt guilt for everything I put her through after...my actions. The dealing. The drugs. I only followed orders, I told myself as the visions of my Uncle Troy telling me about Quincy's death assailed me. While there was peace for a little while, there was also darkness after I left DC. Trice, however, has always been my light. I thought of her when things got tough or whenever we ran out of money. I knew she'd never betray me and accept me with open arms when I returned.

If I had a chance I would turn time around and ask her why she did this to us. I was truly content when I was with her. Not just the physical side, but the togetherness— being with her made me feel like I belonged somewhere. Like someone needed me...depended on me for something. I never had that, and that was something, I guessed, I would always be searching for.

I shook my head and turned my focus on my injury. Lord, it riled me when I saw it. That woman had the nerve to point, aim, and shoot her own son. Thank God it only grazed my arm, whizzing past me. Now, I was aware that Yvonne and I were going to court one week from today- it was a custody hearing. The reason the date was so far away, was for the harsh reality that there was no one who would claim us. We had no contact whatsoever with our relatives, if we had any. Yvonne and I never knew of or met our grandparents. We didn't even know if they were alive. I only remembered, when I was real little, going to an Aunt's funeral with Helen, I also remembered her crying. Something that was abnormal for her.

"Hey Devin. How've you been?" I heard a gentle voice ring; I knew who that was. I started to get up, but she hurried over to me, to lay me back down. The strain had hurt my arm. "Now, I don't want you to hurt yourself." Patrice said softly— like I was a cancer patient. "And I don't expect you to forgive me either."

Maybe if I were to ignore her she'd leave...I had thought about that a long time and then decided to give up on it. I knew her all too well; she wouldn't go.

I sighed and said, "Whatever. I refuse to argue when I'm off my guard. So...shoot. What do want to tell me?" I looked her pointedly in the eye. Her eyes got soggy, and held my hand up and said firmly, "If you're going to cry, then leave. I'm not in the mood for all of that."

I was frowning now, and then she bit her lip and said, "Well...I don't know if I should tell you now...so I won't. I want you to rest. I only came to wish you good luck and...oh-" she swung her large purse off of her shoulder and took out a civics book. I hope it wasn't what I thought it was. "Your homework. Mr. Radford said that, if you needed help with it, then just check your e-mail, and the notes would be there. I can help you if you want-"

"Thank you. I'll take the book home and study or wha tever...just sit it on the chair over there." I said passively.

I hadn't a reason to stay angry with her. If that white dude was who she truly wanted to be with, then so be it. I just hope she knew what she was getting herself into. There was an awkward silence, and I began to tell her to leave when Tyrone walked in.

I smiled and exclaimed, "Yo, man! What up?"

Tyrone came close to the foot of the bed, behind Patrice, and mouthed, "What is she doing here?"

"I don't know." I said aloud. He nodded and sat on the textbook Patrice brought here that was on the chair's surface. We both looked at her with the same thing on our minds...*Get the hell outta' here!* She smiled, kissed my forehead, and left. God, I missed her.

Tyrone grinned and said jokingly, "I heard what y'all was talkin' 'bout. You ain't doin' this work, is you?" He picked up the Civics book and tossed it the next chair.

I scoffed. "Maybe I will, maybe I won't. What you doin' here man?" I asked.

He looked at me as if he was actually appalled and uttered, "I am shocked. I can't be here to support my *amigo* in his time of need? How dare you?"

"Shut up, stupid. Ah!" My arm was giving me trouble again.

I had half a mind to call the nurse for some medicine, when Tyrone blurted out, "So I guess you heard, huh? What people was sayin' around school? She must've told you."

I shook my head and frowned— thinking of that note. What was it that she had to tell me? Was she dying? No, that couldn't be it. "Well," he began and rubbed at his nape, "I don't know if I should tell you man. It ain't my business. You can call her—"

"Hell nah— what is it? If it was that important than she would have the decency to tell me in person. What is it?" I was now desperate to know.

"Man...I just heard it...but...people sayin' she knocked up." I could hear my heart sink in the background.

I gritted my teeth and released, "Oh, shit...that's big. That's...damn it! I'mma fuckin' kill that girl. Damn!" Did she trap me? I knew there was something she was hiding.

I pressed the button that was laying next to me when the nurse's voice chimed, "Yes?"

I panted and said, "Where are my clothes? The ones I came here with?"

"Oh, those? We threw those out honey, but we saved your personal belongings that were inside the pockets and things. Your sister said it was fine to do so, we have some lost and found stuff that would fit you nicely."

"Why'd you throw my clothes away?" I demanded— my arm in pain.

"Well, we would normally hand them back to the owner, but those clothes were covered in blood...we tried washing them, but the stains wouldn't come out. Do you need something, dear?" She asked sweetly.

I sighed in frustration and said, "Yes...I would like everything that was in the pockets of my pants, please." I had to read that note. I thought about it for a moment and added, "And bring some pain killers, too. Thanks."

Nine

IN TUNE WITH NATURE

PASTOR TIM, YVONNE, AND *a woman in a suit had walked in my room with smiles. Except for* Yvonne; she looked sort of pissed. I could understand, though...I still had those homicidal thoughts when I looked at her. That man should be killed...prison was too light a sentence for him. I clenched my fists from the thoughts. I turned my attention to Pastor Tim and greeted his smiling face.

His smile shifted to a gloom expression when he said, "I spoke with Yvonne...and she said that she wanted to be with you. When I heard of what happened I nearly cried. Nothing like that should happen to a child. So, I have made a choice, and I hope you'll accept. Can you tell him the good news, Yvonne?"

Yvonne nodded and turned to look out the window. She sighed and said without looking at me, "He's letting us stay with him until...?" Yvonne glanced at the Pastor sadly and in question.

I was confused when he said, "As long as you two would like. This here," he pointed to the woman that was in a suit and smiling at me. "...is Ms. Lisa Prowl. Your social worker. Now, if you agree to this, then I I'd like for you to tell Ms. Prowl so she can finalize it and tell the judge tomorrow." I nodded and then turned to him in confusion.

"Tomorrow? I thought the court date was in two weeks?"

"And it was. But since I want to claim the two of you, then the date was moved up. Tomorrow. That is when you'll be released from here as well." He nodded and continued, "Well, I guess we'd better go so you can get your rest and recuperation. Let's go Yvonne."

"No. Wait, I want to talk to my sister."

"Okay, that's fine. If you need us we'll be in the waiting room." he said to Yvonne, and then the two of them disappeared. I told her to come closer to me, she did and I kissed her forehead. She was pouting, and very evasive. I hugged her so tightly I knew she couldn't breathe, so I loosened my clutch. It was surprising that she held on to me with the same eagerness that I held her in, but with more desperation. She was hurting my arm, but I didn't care. Yvonne needed me...her big brother...to help her. I could hear her sobbing— could feel her shuddering. I rocked and cooed, but she was still upset in the end. Lord, I needed her to calm down, because when she freaked out so did I, but times ten.

"Vonnie, stop it. It's gonna' be all right from now on. No one's going to hurt you...you're safe with me, baby. You're fine now. Everything's all good." I said almost in tongues it was so rushed. I tried to pull her back and look into those hazel chocolate chips, but she wouldn't let go. It was like she thought I'd evaporate if she were to turn me loose. I patted her back, to comfort her and the mood, and that was when she finally came up to look at me.

"It hurts so much...everything just hurts right now." she whispered.

I turned away to avoid the want to rip the bastard who did that to her head off of his shoulders. The need to hurt him was still a strong thought and notion overcoming my mindset. I needed to distract myself, but how? With Yvonne this way I doubted if I could get her on the subject of Christmas; a time of bliss.

"Yvonne, how long has this been going on? What has he been doing to you? The ugly guy— Mom's boyfriend?"

She was sniffling when she replied, "Vincent! He's...I don't know..." she sobbed. My face took on a sternness I never knew I could muster.

"Yvonne stop crying, now! You've got to be strong through it all, if you cry now it would give him victory. He's winning, Vonnie, I don't think I like that." she looked as though she saw the light, so I continued, "You're stronger than that."

She swallowed, "I needed that. Thanks Dev."

"Anytime." I replied. She was looking at me with a weird expression. I braced myself and then asked, "Are you okay? I mean, you seemed so isolated...are you upset with me? Do you feel as though I failed you as your big brother? Just tell me— I can take it." My words were as true as the birthmark on my thigh. Yvonne, miraculously smiled from ear-to-ear and said, "Why would you ask me something as dumb as that?"

"Yvonne just answer the—"

"Really? You should already know the answer to that. If it wasn't for you I wouldn't be here today." I looked at her, amazed, and said, "What do you mean by that?"

"Here's your belongings Mr. Cooper." the nurse entered our conversation as she did the room, with an annoying voice and everything that was in my pockets of my jeans: my keys, some loose change... a folded piece of notebook paper.

"Have a nice day you guys." she welcomed.

"Thanks!" Yvonne and I said in unison. We stared at each other, I broke my gaze by snatching my attention away and to the note. I breathed hard, and my hands trembled while trying to unfold it. "What's that—"

"A note!" I answered her quickly so I could open it without the guilt of having to explain. I unscrambled it, and read the beautiful sprawling in awe:

Hey Devin.

How you doin?

How's Yvonne?

~~I was just wondering if you were free tonight No! I ain't mean that, alright? But, really, do you need somebody to go with you to the dance on Fri~~

Never mind that, I'm writing in pen and it's really not doing any justice. But, for real, boo, um, Devin— remember that guy you saw that came out of my house last week? Well, funny story, his name was Archer...one of my Mom's patients. He came over because my mother told him to, and when he got there he found out she wasn't home. It was just me alone. I let him come in because I noticed when I started talking to him, that he had a disorder that...uh...what was that word? Impaired? Yeah, it impaired his speech and he...basically had the mind of a six-year old. I was afraid that if he were to walk home he'd stand in the middle of traffic or something and kill himself. Since he seemed so innocent, I didn't want that happening. Archer said his Mom would pick him up later, so he decided that he wanted to sit on the porch and wait for her. I said he could, and I went to sit in the living room to watch over him— in case he strayed. Well, from there I guess you know the rest.

I guess you heard the rumors, huh? That everyone keeps saying that I'm pregnant, and I feel the need to tell you, personally, that I am. There is something else I should tell you...it's actually quite important. I do not think you are the FATHER! I will not tell you who I think it is, but all I'm saying is this:

I still love you.

I didn't think my jaw would ever snap close, again. There were only three words running through my head: *what the hell?*

Ten

Testify

"I WAS JUST TRYING to protect my babies!" Helen said helplessly. What an actor. It was the day of court and the beginning of a D.F.H. (day from hell). Helen was called to the stand to testify against her naysayers. It was a small hearing, only I, Pastor Tim, Yvonne, and Helen were present. Ms. Prowl was there beside me, as was the Pastor. Judge Jergins sat his desk and listened to Helen's lies in sternness. It was apparent that her story was moving no one.

"See, Vincent and I were arguing and it just got a little out of control, but nothing bad ever happened. I mean, I went in my room to take a nap, and I told him to make himself at home. After I said that, I woke up and heard all this screaming so I grabbed my gun and handled— you know— my business." she said with the victimized expression.

Why should she be feeling that way?

"Okay, so where did you get the gun from Ms. Cooper?" Jergins inquired.

Her eyes got really wide and she looked as though she would slug him. "H-How dare you...it was my late husband's...sir." I could see it took some restraint in saying what she did. I just wished that she would fess up and be over with it. Just let the penal system run its course with that weirdo. "Listen...sir. I love him— I ain't want nothing happening to my baby. D-Devin, baby, t-tell them what I did to try to— I wanted to save you! Vonnie...tell them what mommy did...I tried to help her— them. Oh...Vince wasn't doing anything to her, believe him! I swear when I walked through the door I was scared, because I saw Devin beating on him like he...please judge— just believe me! I don't want to go to jail..." she was sobbing now.

The sheriff took her to her seat next to her lawyer. I turned to her and she smiled at me— a sly smile. I flared my nostrils, widened my eyes and began shaking. I tried to control myself, but was getting nowhere. I knew nothing would work unless I were to—

"You son of—" I growled and stood from my chair to start for her. I was held back by someone; I didn't care for who it was. I just knew that that person wasn't strong enough to keep me away from her. Helen was moving back and gasping— feigning her astonishment. I was pounding the air nearing her, not the actual her. When I cocked my head around, I was not surprised by what was going on; it had taken two men to hold me back: Pastor Tim and the bailiff. Well, I was already breaking free of their embraces anyway, so it didn't do any real justice to my physical standard. It did, however, make me realize how much I was harming myself. If I were to harm Helen in any way it would make me a hypocrite. Rendering me no better than the ugly dude who...the man who violated my family. And there was no way I would lower myself to such standards.

"It's not worth it son, she's not worth it. Just let it go and tell your story." I whipped around to Pastor Tim, his hand was on my shoulder, ushering me back to my seat. I was panting and she was still smiling while the judge was watching us all in disbelief. I get even angrier.

Well, all in all, Pastor Tim is approved for temporary custody and everyone goes on with their lives. Helen goes to prison for seven years, for attempted manslaughter, and the ugly dude goes right along with her, but for a longer sentence I didn't care too much about.

Getting something that you cannot have
Respecting choices but not wanting to mix
Always daring to be different with nothing in particular
Yet knowing the world will not accept the fix.

-Devin Cooper

Eleven

THE PHILOSOPHY OF CHANGE

"*WILL YOU PLEASE PASS the bread, Devin?" Sylvia said to me in a gentle monotone. It was* dinnertime in the Blake household, and Yvonne and I were pretty much forced to join. We were living with the Blake's for about a week and a half with a great supply of love! No, really, I just wasn't feeling it; the fact that we were actually here...a haven? Some sort of safe place? I felt secure here, but never really adjusted. Yvonne was a mute, moping around the house and doing things in the subnormal and numbness. It killed me to see her that way, but I saw that there was nothing more I could do.

"Sure," I agreed, and did as Sylvia wished; the bread was now in her possession.

It was a Wednesday, and there it was— my first day back to Hades. I spent the last days of my recuperation at "home" with the Blake's. I gained like ten pounds, and got taller (I think), so the excess weight was unnoticeable. I was dragged to the mall to get new clothes, I hated shopping a great deal, it wasn't manly and just not my scene. I almost forgot about my hair; my hair had grown to an extraordinary length, it was in cornrows now but looked, to me, like dreads. It reached halfway down my elongated arm and now...I was self considered a giant freak with new gear and an irritating hairdo.

It all came to a surprise to me that Sylvia attended Easton Rogue. I never saw her, never heard of her, and never once considered the thought of her going to such a ghetto school with low standards. It was funny, because she said she saw me around a few times before but never had the "guts to talk to me". Well, I guess life was full of surprises and expiration dates.

Pastor Tim gave us a lift to school, we both exited the car, wished him a good day and walked inside of what I didn't think of to be a battlefield of gazes. I turned to Sylvia, who had her head down, and decided since there was no turning back, then I might as well go through with it with a smile on my face. Enter with confidence. "Caucasian persuasion!" "What is she doin' with a fine dude like that?" "Is that Devin with a white girl?" "I feel so sorry for him..."

I couldn't take the pressure, so I rushed to my locker that was on the other side of school; after all, Sylvia Janice Blake was a freshman.

I was a sophomore. Bam, our worlds divided.

Well, I guessed living with the Blake's was a vacation for me. A getaway from the shit that normally went on in my life. I tried as hard as my mind could allow to forget about Trice and her...situation. I felt like an ass, but at the same time I thought, was it the right thing to dump her? For that reason? Even though she had confessed to me that she had been cheating? I was just confused all the time now. I didn't know whether if I were coming or going.

School had let out, and it was then when it hit me. A realization that was so very clear now, it made me want to double over in laughter: it was October.

Halloween was coming up, and in the Masters household it was a major event. We would all dress up and go around the good stores in New York, resulting in large sums of sweets and treats. It was never the best thing to follow tradition, and skulk around houses asking for candy. My best bet would be a firm reprimand, and a lingering fear factor. This was why one could never trust what they saw on the television; walking around and asking for candy door-to-door was only glamorized by the media. Living in the hood had its effects— taking this advice from me would be wise. I was hardened because of the streets.

It was a weird agreement, I know, but I agreed to sleep in the basement. The Pastor urged me to take the room he had set up for me...what was it called again? Oh, the "guest room." He said he'd put Yvonne in Sylvia's room, and that room was for me. I declined and made a room for myself in the lower level of their home. The basement. I was in the process of building it— my space. A Devin Cooper area where I could just chill with the doors locked. It was cool, because there were already major appliances in there: a sink, a mini fridge, and the extra washing machine, but I was unsure if I could use that or not. Knowing the Pastor, he'd probably say yes, but it would be in my best interest to ask him first, though.

I was laying in bed downstairs, when I heard my name being called.

"Yes?" I called back. It was Mrs. Blake. She was almost as tall as me, which was surprising, with strong arms and a sweet personality. Any dude who'd take advantage of her was inhumane. She was such a sweetheart that when she'd call me to take the trash out I'd feel as if I'd committed a crime if I refused. "May I speak with you for a moment?"

"Yes, ma'am." I agreed and started up the steps. She had a big smile on her face and that made me smile, too. I was scratching my hair when she looked up at it and said gently, "Come on." She ushered me to the dining room tables, we both sat eye to eye. Her face shifted from warm and gentle to business. That made me edgy. "How would you feel about...cutting your hair?" I nodded, taking it in. I felt the braids in my hair. Would I be able to do that? This hair was a large chunk of my life.

My past. And to cut it off would be like murdering my past life. I was always threatening to cut it...but I never carried through with the plan. I couldn't even imagine myself with it gone...my mane. Besides, my hair was giving her no problems at all. "Does my hair bother you?"

"Oh. No! I was just asking, because I thought it bothered you."

"Why would you think that?" I asked. I held my hand up, "Never mind."

I stopped the deliberation and said quickly, before I changed my mind, "That would be a great idea. Yes, thank you."

After all, I was stripping away as much of the past as I could.

Twelve

THE BLISS OF LIGHT

WHEN PASTOR TIM WAS *finished shaving my hair away, I was quickly sent to the* bathroom to admire it. It felt so clean. There was a breeze that was combing through my mowed bands of hair. I massaged it with a longing for what it used to be. I had to forget about that, though. New hair. New scene. New Devin. Right?

I decided to go show Yvonne before the mirror, though I knew she'd probably lie about its badness, I wanted her to see it first anyway. I was about to knock when I heard her talking to someone. I knew it wasn't a dude, I would've noticed it. It was a trill voice instead. Sylvia Blake. There was a crack in the door so I placed my ear there and eavesdropped.

"...I wanted to tell him but I don't know. What do you think I should do?" Yvonne was saying to Sylvia. She sighed, "Well...I don't have much experience with boys. But I do know this, you tell Russell how you feel no matter how stupid it may sound. You said he told you he...loves you?"

Yvonne paused and I supposed she nodded. "So you should tell him that you do, as well. You shouldn't lie to yourself." Sylvia breathed and added, "Trust me. I know the feeling of wanting to tell somebody you love them, but never having the chance. It's... hard to explain."

"No, it's not." Yvonne said doggedly. "Just tell it girl. Tell me who you're crushing on. I told you my crush." Was this still my little sister talking?

"Well, I don't know. It's just...I'm shy. I'll describe him to you. He is very tall, with long hair, tan skinned, and pretty eyes."

"Do I know him?" Yvonne asked anxiously.

"As a matter of fact, he—"

Their conversation was interrupted with the sound of my hard knock on the door. "Knock, knock! Can I come in ladies?"

"Okay!" both of them said in sync. Yvonne stumbled over to the door and answered with a frantic expression. "W-What do you, whoa—" she stuttered. I looked at her in curiosity, and remembered that my hair was hacked off.

"I like the new haircut, Devin." Sylvia said from the bed.

I looked at her quickly, then back to Yvonne. My heart was pounding so fast my thoughts couldn't keep pace, and the compliment killed me. "Thank you, Blake. Um,

I came to ask what you guys thought about my haircut. Do you like it? Do I look like a mutant from hell?"

"No!" they both yelped together. The atmosphere was awkward so I turned the other way and left. What the hell was that? This was freaking me out. I could not believe that I overheard something so vile. How could Yvonne do this? Like someone? No, love someone? It was horrible to hear such things. And what was Sylvia doing in her room anyway? She was no good, and was not going to influence my innocent little sister. After all the things she'd been through— that *we* had been through— there was no way I would condone this. Sylvia giving Yvonne advice would surely stop.

I went to the bathroom, glanced at my haircut, and strode nonchalantly to the basement. I was now weary for some reason. Maybe it was all the thinking I had been doing. Maybe it was just the nerves— I wouldn't know.

There was nothing to do! I was fired from my job at the pizza joint before I could even begin working there, and Tyrone was always home with Sasha and the kids nowadays. I had nowhere to go. Nowhere to be. No one to see.

Nothing to do.

It was probably for the best though.

Thirteen

All in Good Will

"May I go out?" *I asked Mrs. Blake, unaware of what the answer would turn out to be. Again,* Mrs. Blake took on this serious expression for her gentle features and ushered me to the dining room table. She folded her arms across her chest and leaned back. Then she eased off of the brakes and placed her elbows on the table. Husky style.

"Devin...you know about Sylvia, right? Do you?" she asked suspiciously. Damn, so much for innocence. "It's pretty personal."

"No. I have no idea what you're talking about." I said plainly.

"Well Sylvia has a little crush...well..." she contemplated.

"What? What are you talking about?" I asked her. It wasn't like I was asking to go out on a date with Sylvia—we all knew that was implausible. I tried to avoid the prior realization of that fact. I knew what she was think-ing about, and the matter was more than a little, "crush." Sylvia Blake was very obvious. I noticed the times when I would walk passed her in school, she'd duck her head and blush. I might be bored, but not stupid. Virgins were so cute. "Sylvia and I have had a little talk about physical relations and proper precautions...now the reason I ask you these questions are because...well have you been having the same thoughts as she has? About the relations and attractions between..." I wanted to guffaw in her face. And I immediately regretted it after it was done. She looked at me as if I were crazy, and I stood, headed toward the door, and walked out. I had to do this. Besides, it was sort of insulting for her to think that I was still a virgin. Hence, the laughter.

I had to walk everywhere I went now, because I lent my car out to Tyrone. It wasn't like I could drive it now- with this cast on my arm. I remember he asked me for it until the baby came in another week or so. I reluctantly condoned and now I was walking my way to his apartment building. It wasn't far, so it was no problem getting there.

It was apartment 3-C, I found it, and a short, swollen, woman answered. She was smoking a cigarette, and smiling at me. "Who the hell are you?" she mumbled with the cig in her mouth. I wasn't surprised she didn't recognize me. "Sasha, it's me. Devin Cooper...I roll with Ty and 'em. We met last month." She eyed me down for a long moment and shrugged. "I don't remember you— Ty gotta' lot of homies. You could be just another face." she blew smoke in my nostrils and I inhaled deeply, missing the taste of nicotine. She began to shut the door, when the sound of a booming voice shook the surface. "Sasha! Who's at the door?" Tyrone's voice was unmistakable. He came to the door and laughed goofily and loudly. Sasha demanded silence for the children's sake, and stomped back into the apartment— Tyrone's glare stalking her on the way. He came out and laughed anyway, but shut the door.

"Yo, what up man? I ain't see you in, like, three weeks. How you been?"

I shrugged. "Been...chillin.'"

"That's good." he began to frown, but scratched the back of his head. I sighed and began, "What now?"

"I ain't wanna' say nothing', but Trice...that girl is a HO! I thought you knew already."

"I don't think I want to know. Is it bad?" I asked sarcastically. Knowing it was.

He nodded and said, "I actually heard two things...first, Trice says she been creepin' with Jack Burn."

"Who is that?"

"You don't know? Man, that nigga' go hard core! The dude in the, um, 590 gang. But check it, his crew got mad beef with you, man. I can get some people to help you out—"

"All right— what about bad news number two?"

"Oh, yeah...um...was you really sleepin' with Ms. Sanchez? I mean, it was just what I heard from around." He turned away and said, "Let's go for a walk."

"Why can't you drive?" He looked away with a solemn expression that filled me with trepidation. Where the hell was my ride? I thought in panic. If I were to allow the usage of my car to another, then I expected that person to have the decency to return my personal belongings! "Ty...where the hell is my shit?" I continued. "Don't play, man." I warned him wryly.

We just kept walking until he said, "That's where we headed man, to go get your ride." There was no sign of humor on his face as he said the words to me.

I turned away from the gargantuan, and mumbled. "Who got it, yo?" When I turned back around to see him, because his pause had been prolonged, he was rubbing the bulge in his side pocket. My eyes widened, and then I mentally composed myself, the external in delay. The day was slowly escalating into darkness when we reached a shaggy trap house on the corner. When I got there, I noticed a silver, old fashioned-looking car that made me want to jump for joy. It was my car. I did not care if it was old-looking or not— it was mine. The last remaining piece of New York that I had with me. There was no way I was giving that up. Surprisingly, the keys were in the ignition, and I opened the door and hopped in. Tyrone had a scarf over his mouth, and there was a clicking noise that was noticeable.

Tyrone had a gun.

When I initially saw it I cringed, and frowned. He was sneaking into the house, when I hissed, "Get your stupid ass over here! We got the car, now let's roll! What you got a gun for?" He was crouching when he turned, "Just stay there, all right? This nigga, owe me some money. I'll be right out." he pulled his scarf down and chuckled lowly, "Yo, man— I'll be a'ight. Trust me..." at that moment, I guess he knew what would happen to him. He must've been real sure to tell me that. He was so quiet sneaking in, I hadn't noticed he left.

A few minutes later, it sounded as if there was war going on inside the trap house. A man came running out, jumped in my car. It was Tyrone, he gasped, "Drive, man!" I hit the gas and the car was reluctant to move. It was too dark to see if there was gas in the tank or not, but the car spoke for itself. I was panicking when men came rushing out of the house with weapons, like guns and knives. Finally, the car accelerated down the street. I had no idea where I was going, but instinct warned me to keep driving with my one hand. We were now in the boondocks, and I realized it was safe to park. Tyrone had been silent on the drive up there and it worried me. "Ty...yo, you hear me?" he didn't answer. I shook him, he moaned, and said, "Yo, man I told your stupid ass not to worry...yo, I can hook you up if...remember the time when we robbed that concession stand...? That shit was...funny..." he coughed up blood, and I knew where he was going.

Tyrone lolled his head back against the passenger seat, there was a dark blotch on the front of his wife-beater, and I put the car in gear and drove to the hospital. "Hang in there man." I breathed sadly. His breathing was strained and his last words became a ringing in my ears.

"Trust me man...I'll be all right."

Fourteen

CODE ORANGE

I TOLD THE POLICE where we were and how everything went down. I wasn't a snitch, but this was for the justice of my dead friend. So, screw a Jack Burn and his gang of thugs and gorillas, I just wanted everything to end well.

Sasha and the kids didn't take the news well. It was a shame that they didn't have enough to pay for a proper funeral. His parents had money, so I bet they'd take care of that themselves. Sasha, and the kids, were moving with her parents in Maryland, so they had very few financial problems.

In school the next day, Tyrone's business was announced for the school to hear:

"Students. Staff. Everyone. I have very sad news for you guys today. Yesterday a student of ours was fatally shot. However, the police have taken in the murderers after finding them trying to flee the area. We will all miss and remember you,

Tyrone Zelman. You will be in our hearts. Counseling services are available today during all lunch hours..."

Now that little announcement was enough to set me off. Principal Hammin hadn't even known who Ty was. You couldn't grieve for him if you didn't know him. Tyrone was one of a kind soldier. He took care of his own and manned his shit. And for that, I saluted him.

I was excused from class to use the restroom. Although, I think it was clear to everyone that I didn't want to be there. I was just numb now. After what happened to Tyrone...I was just dried up. I didn't have it in me to fight it. I just couldn't hang on anymore. There wasn't any strength left to have an "emotional breakdown." I had pondered the fact of whipping the principal's ass, but decided not to and left. I had no car as of now, so I started to walk home. Well, not home, because I didn't have one to go to. I've lived in many houses, but never a home. New York was where my heart was. I would go back there if the chance was within reach. Too bad I had only hope left to my name. Otherwise I would've been out of here.

I had nowhere to go, so I began northern bound. I ended up inside of a Mini Mart, where I bought a bag of tortillas and a can of Pepsi. As I was paying for it though, the clerk was watching me with lustful eyes. I smiled back at her advances. "Hello, cutie." I said to her. She blushed and handed my bagged items over to me. I chuckled, and headed for the door. "Hey, wait!" she called out to me. Her GRAY eyes alight with mischief. She began to look around, we were the only two inside the store. "Come here! My boss won't be here for another half an hour. Come on!" I shrugged, and followed her to the restroom. It was the only way to take my mind off the negative.

* * *

Ten minutes later, I left with a smile, a phone number, and an open armed welcome for the next visit. I had no morals, I guessed, and that was why I probably did something so spontaneous. I considered the possibility of getting help...but there was no way that I was getting my head shrank. I mean, I had some sort of decency to admit that I had a problem, not many people can look at themselves and admit things— true things. To take the time to sit down and own up to their addictions or bad habits, was something that set me aside from the rest.

Thinking of it now, I was sort of tired of the same scene. I needed a change. I had to face the truth and the truth was: I didn't want to live with Blake's any longer. They were a nice crowd but a little too nice for my style. I was walking somberly to my destination when it hit me. I just realized that living with the Blake's was a simple, yet temporary, change of key. I really didn't know how Yvonne felt about the whole thing, but I knew it was a lifestyle I no longer desired. And I thought I wanted the "all American home"when it turned out that it was the last experience I needed. Besides, living there had pushed me away from reality and the streets. And that was who I was. I stopped in front of the beautiful blue house and jammed my hands into my pockets. I felt for my lighter and took it out, along with my cigarettes. I lit it, sat on a stone nearby, and glared at it. That house. The epitome of all the hurt, the pain, the harsh memories. I hadn't a single reason to care for that house, Helen was a part of it. Her spirit was still attached to the damn thing. I looked at its beauty and cringed. Why should something so beautiful still stand? Be seen by the world of its loveliness, while I look at it and shudder from the pain? When painted faces would walk by and admire its splendor, while this shadow glared at it and spat at its true ugliness? Why should the shadow suffer? I took a long drag from my cig and threw it at the front door. The flame hit the furry doormat and small flames came from the artificial makeup. My eyes bulged and I ran, like hell down the street. After all, old habits die hard.

Before I knew it, I was back at the house I wanted to leave the most and smiling in Pastor Tim's face. He looked at me in concern and then said, "School's out already? Why, it's only two forty-five." I nodded and he grabbed my arm and whispered in my ear. "We have a guest, son." I feigned a grin and scanned the empty premises. Why did I need to know that? I didn't care, I think he needed to understand that. I shrugged him off, he didn't notice, and he showed me to the living room. There was a tall Mrs. Blake speaking with a woman with long red hair, and an hourglass figure. Pastor Blake cleared his voice to establish that he wanted attention, the two looked up and their eyes, simultaneously, went to me. Well, of course, I thought, there's a black guy standing in the middle of the living room with a bad attitude. Who wouldn't look? "Mary, Brenda, this is the new edition to our family, Devin."

"How do you do?" The woman named Brenda greeted me. She extended her hand out to me, I shook it. Although I never engage myself in such formal greetings.

"This is our niece, Brenda Walsh who just came in from Ohio. She is attending college there, and came here for Christmas just to visit the family. She's only staying for...three weeks?" the statement was asking Brenda.

"Two weeks." She answered "I'm spending Christmas with my parents in Massachusetts, but I'd love to stay longer."

"Well, sadly, she must go early, because of exams, but with the little time we have her— we'll be sure to enjoy her. Devin, why don't you show her to her room." I turned to look him in the eye with, I supposed a pleading look on my face. "Where would that be?" I was just wondering that, since Yvonne and I had taken all the rooms. He grinned at me as if I were crazy and was supposed to know where the room was, and said, "Yvonne and Brenda will be sharing the guest room." I thought about it for a moment. The guest room was only enough space for one, how would the two of them sleep? While I had an entire floor to myself downstairs? Something needed to be changed. "Well, Yvonne can sleep downstairs with me. I have more than enough room." I offered. Pastor Tim thought about it. "It wouldn't hurt. Brenda how do you feel about that?" Brenda shrugged. "We'll wait until Yvonne comes home, and ask her. We cool?"

I chuckled and agreed. "We cool."

"So, here it is." I said to her with a shrug. I placed her bags on the bed and headed for the door. No need to stay any longer, I knew when my services were needed no longer. I only made it to the steps when she called me back inside the room.

"Uh, yes?"

What could she want? I went inside and she eyed me up and down. "I wanted to ask you something. Can you shut the door?" I did as she asked. This was when I started to worry. She sat on the bed, and waved for me to sit beside her, I did. "How are you?"

"Pretty good. I'm, uh, pretty gucci."

She looked at me with curiosity, shrugged and said. "Okay, I'm just gonna' come out and ask you this. Have you been with...Sylvia? My cousin? Aunt Mary put me up to it. I'm sorry for asking you."

"Why does she keep suspecting that? Why would I want to do anything with a little girl? Why in the hell does she keep asking me that? It's sick."

Brenda was glaring at me. "What? Are you calling my cousin sick? What did she ever do to you?" This hostility threw me off. What the...

"No, I was just saying—"

"Well, I'm just saying— get out of my room!" she demanded. To refrain from saying anything rash, I stood up and started for the door. "Go! Now!" she ordered, her voice almost screaming.

"I'm leaving!"

"Well, you're not moving fast enough for me!"

I stormed out and she slammed the door behind me. What the fuck was wrong with these Blake women? One accuses me with sleeping with her daughter, the daughter keeps coming on to me, and that new one was just downright insane. I tell her the truth and all of a sudden she gets all fatal attraction on me. That damn family was just crazy as hell. Shoot, offered her the better room and she dumps on me. I'm glad I took Yvonne out of there then. I didn't want her lashing out on her for no reason, as she did me.

Fifteen

FATHER

I COULDN'T JUST IGNORE the fact that Patrice told me she was pregnant. Nor could I ignore the fact that I had burned a house down, and that it was all over the news. Pastor Tim and his wife were watching it, saying silent prayers for whoever was hurt. "Golly," the Pastor said. "What sort of monster would commit such a sin." I looked down and swore.

"What was that Devin?" Brenda said to me- she was testing me. The bitch.

"Nothing." I said with a false smile and happiness, because the entire family was looking me directly in the eye.

I was sitting on the love seat alongside Yvonne. And on the next two chairs sat the older Blake's, and on the other were Brenda and Sylvia. The two looked totally different from each other. Brenda was the taller, older, redhead with an attitude as fiery as her hair, and Sylvia was the shorter, younger, golden child of the Blake's. Well, all that didn't matter then, because I knew I would be facing fifteen to life in the big house soon.

"Neighbors say that they saw someone last night, in black, but they could not make out the identity of the culprit. It was the home of twenty nine year-old Helen Cooper. Where she lived with her sixteen-year-old son, Devin Cooper and twelve-year-old daughter, Yvonne Masters. Thankfully no one was hurt, but many prayers go out to the family."

All eyes were on the two of us, Yvonne and I. I looked down and I saw the girl cry and cling to me. I hugged and cooed her, but her cries never ceased.

"It'll be all right, little one. I understand—" Pastor Tim started.

"No it's not! You don't understand what it's like to lose your mom and your dad. How could you possibly understand that!" Yvonne shouted. Her large, brown ponytail was hiding my face, and the guilt that was evident there. She stood and trudged to the basement. I guess I was the only one who could really talk to her and 'understand'. Especially since that was my room she stormed into. I looked at everyone and proclaimed, "I apologize. I'll talk to her." I walked up to the basement door and twisted the knob. It was stuck— it was locked. I pulled at the door, it wouldn't budge, so I called out to her. "Vonnie, open the door!" There was no response. I raised my voice a little. "Yvonne, open the door, now!"

The door was unlocked, and I stepped inside. I heard Brenda say behind me, "What a brute." I ignored it and continued inside. I shut the door behind me, started down the steps, and saw her on my bed crying. I sat next to her and gave her a bear hug. It usually made her feel better, but not this time. I probably sat there for thirty minutes straight, not saying anything, she was just weeping. By the time she recovered, Mrs. Blake called from upstairs that dinner was ready. I looked at Yvonne, she didn't meet my eyes. "You wanna' go eat?"

She shook her head. "I don't have much of an appetite right now."

"Well, you can't just sit here and not eat. Go put something in your stomach." I told her. She nodded, stood, and left. I told her I would meet her up there in a few. I needed some time to think. I thought on it for a long time, whether I should turn myself in or not. What else would I do in the future? I had no future. A nobody like me would probably end up in jail with ten bastard kids that I denied anyway. What did life have in store for me? Without Yvonne I would've been in jail already, for hate crimes. I had to think on it longer. Too bad that wasn't in the question, because Mrs. Blake warned me that my plate was getting cold, and I was kind of hungry.

When I arrived upstairs, everyone kept their heads low, and avoided my eyes. Everyone except Yvonne. I smiled at her and sat down. It was a quiet dinner, while it lasted. When it was over, we all departed and placed our plates in the sink, and left. Everyone went their different directions.

I was in bed downstairs, in the dark. I was actually woken by a small body beside me. Yvonne. It was my cuddling little sister, who I loved so much. She shifted, I wrapped my arms around her , and drifted off to sleep. Minutes later, I guessed, I was awaken with...a kiss? Yvonne? That was when I realized:

Whoever this was— was not my little sister.

I was unconsciously kissing this person back; of course, I was a guy after all. I felt lips and I moved with them. I gained consciousness and pushed her away.

"Who the hell is this?" I hissed in the darkness. She didn't answer, kept kissing me. I kissed her deeper and pushed her away, I had to realize that, whoever this was...it was wrong to do this. I wasn't a home wrecker. "Sylvia, get out!" I took a shot in the dark by saying her name— literally. I grabbed hold of her body...and felt that she was naked. I almost lost control. I swallowed hard and said, "Leave. Now."

"Why? Devin...I thought you liked me."

"Well, I don't. Go!" I ordered, a little louder this time. She flinched and went stiff. "So I guess you really don't like my cousin, do you?"

My eyes widened when I realized that it wasn't Sylvia but—

That person was Brenda Walsh.

Sixteen

WHAT MY TEACHER TAUGHT ME

"So...IT WAS A FALSE alarm?" I asked my ex girlfriend, Patrice, over the phone. I realized that I couldn't just block the problem out any longer. She told me that she was pregnant three weeks ago...and it seemed as if it were forever. I still remembered that day...when Ty told me...and when she told me...that was the worst day of my life.

"Well," she began. "I'm still pregnant, but...like I said...I do not think you're the father. I stop taking my pill right around the time I...got with Burn. So...you don't even need to concern yourself with that. How you been? What are you up to?"

"Pretty good, beside the fact that my mother tried to kill me, my arm still hurts, and that the family I stay with is crazy, I'm fine." Was what I wanted to say, but said, "Nothing much," instead. "Just gettin' ready for church. I kinda' have to...now that I live with a Pastor and what not. It's not bad, though sometimes I wish I didn't have to wake up so early to get ready and go." I sighed. It was becoming difficult. I never once thought that I would be discussing church with Patrice Newbern. But, hey, some things could change- right? "I, um, actually called and wanted to know if you would like to come— to church, I mean." As soon as the words escaped my lips I regretted them. I felt like such a damn dork. She was thinking about it.

"I don't know, Devin. I wouldn't want to impose..."

"What would you be imposing on? The more I recruit for church, the better, right?" It was sort of true.

"I guess," she said pointedly. "What time should I be there?" She asked. I thought about it. We were leaving for Sunday school, so I thought it would be right for her to come for service instead. It just fit.

"How about ten?"

"Sounds good to me. I'll see you there."

"All right. Bye." I hung up. Did I just invite Patrice Newbern to church? The girl who broke my heart? I just hoped that all hell wouldn't break loose in a holy place.

It really sucked that my car was impounded. Although, it wasn't like I could drive it anyway, my hand was busted. However, I was riding to church with the crazies, and was sure to place myself nearest toward the window. I refrained from sitting close to a Blake.

Or the Walsh.

Yvonne was sick, emotionally as well as physically, so she decided not attend with us all. God, how I missed her. I needed someone to sit next to right now instead of one of the three psycho woman in the Blake car.

When we unloaded the car, I nearly ran inside the building. Eager to escape one of the three women as fast as I could. With speed comes joy. I found my seat in the sanctuary, secluded, but I was followed. By Sylvia this time. I scooted away from her, but she moved with me. I scooted until I could move no further, and hissed, "What do you want?" I kept my eyes straight ahead. If I did more than that, Mrs. Blake would've taken it as intercourse. Her suspicions were starting to annoy me. Sylvia looked up at me and said, "You are the...ugh...the densest person I know. It's as plain as day that my cousin likes you." she shook her head and said, "What a jack." I looked at her in shock. I had never heard her swear before. It was a first for me. I smirked and said, "Oh yeah? What about you? I thought you were the one who had the hots for me." She rolled her eyes and swallowed. "Oh, get over yourself. I just wanted to have sex with you, but you were the one making it so difficult." she eyed me down. "You're still cute though." This little girl was just a big ball of surprise. Things were just unraveling as time passed. I snorted. "What do you want from me? The moon?"

"Maybe." she challenged.

"Well, I'm no superman." I eyed her down. " And you damn well ain't no Lois Lane." I had to get hood on that one. She shrugged, rolled her eyes, and admitted, "Too bad that wasn't what I came for. I wanted you to ask Brenda out."

"You mean on a date?"

"Duh? Where else would you take her?"

"The loony bin." I muttered.

"What was that?" she demanded lowly.

I smiled, "Oh, nothing. Just a whole lotta' nothing." there was no way I was taking her anywhere. "There's no way I'm taking her anywhere." I verbalized. "I thought this might happen. Well...I have a lot of dirt on you Mr. Cooper. A lot." she said maniacally. I turned to her real fast.

"Like what? Let me guess, I didn't 'take out the garbage'?"

She shook her head, "You're just adding on to the list aren't you?" she continued. "I'm talking about...last night. You and Brenda were downstairs doing-"

"You wouldn't!" I said sarcastically. She really wasn't getting to me. "Not to be rude girl, but I frankly don't give a damn." I stood and swaggered away, still eager to leave as I had entering the place. I stopped in my tracks when she hissed, "What about Patrice Newbern? It's all over school—"

"Shut up!" I said to her a bit too loudly. "That isn't any of your concern."

"Well, take my cousin out then." she raised her voice. I walked up to her and glared... I had no other choice. "Fine. I'll do it." I barked. That bitch was blackmailing me. What did I ever do to her? And why was she in my business anyway? Sylvia stood, adjusted her dress, and started down the aisle. She turned back and said, loud enough for the small group of people in the sanctuary to hear, "Oh, and, happy birthday Devin!" Before I could think about it, the group began to clap for me, standing up from seats and wishing me a happy birthday.

"You look great, I'm glad you could make it." I was telling Patrice as I was walking her to her car. It was true, I wouldn't lie about something like that. Her skin was smooth and radiant, teeth as bright as her attitude. When we made it to her car, she buckled herself inside, and I stood by her window. "Oh, wait. I got you something." Patrice reached toward the back seat of the passenger seat and handed me a small bag. "What's this?" I frowned. I was seriously confused. It was her turn to frown this time. "What are you talking about? Just open the bag." I did, and there was about twenty little chocolates inside. "Chocolate?" I questioned. What could be so special? "Keep looking." She urged. I looked deeper inside and saw a silver bracelet that read, "To Someone Special" on its front. It felt a little weird, receiving a gift like that from a girl, but I took it. I looked at her in surprise, and she gave me a look that said to keep looking. I discovered a card that read:

HAPPY BIRTHDAY

On the front. I opened it up and saw the note that she wrote on the second flap:

"I wish you a very happy birthday
I hope we can still be friends
I hope all your wishes come true
Although we're not together
You'll always be my boo"
-Trice

I looked at her and smiled. I gave her that smile that said: Of course I'll be your friend. I gave her a kiss on the cheek, a friendly kiss, her engine revved, she drove forward. She stopped before she drove completely out of the parking area, peeped her head out the window and gushed, "Tell Yvonne I said 'hey'. All right?"

"Yeah. Thank you." I hated to admit it, but I really did miss her.

On the drive home, I stared out the window and thought of what things would be like if I had the mind-set of the past. I thought about it for a long time, and what if I had let Trice explain all those months ago? If I had just came at a different time, to her house, would my life be any better? Would I be in this ordeal? Living with weirdos? Would Ty still be alive?

"What do you get when you mix black and white together?" Sylvia asked me, her blue eyes filled with a curiosity that made me hella uncomfortable. I shrugged, partially as an answer to that random ass question and a conveyance of my actual confusion.

"Hell if I know," I told her because hell, I really didn't. "Why is the sky blue?"

We stood against the brick wall just outside Easton Rogue High and were in the middle of laughing at some geeky-looking kid I vaguely recognized from Spanish class fall to the ground.

It was sort of...unconventional, our relationship. Since meeting in that holy place we made it a point to pick up as many bad habits as possible. At least I did. I made it my mission to expose the sheltered church girl to the ways of the world, so to speak, and one of those ways involved heavy indica and ditching out on those useless classes.

"Oh, crap!" The tiny white girl gasped after choking on the blunt. "Devin look! He's falling."

I barely get the words out before I see the Geeky Kid Kid continue to roll down the grassy hill he fell down. But it ain't exactly a clumsy fall he took, I notice, as the three guys stroll into view seconds after. They're howling by the time Geeky Kid reaches the bare bottom of the patch where a shit ton of mud rests. He's covered in the goo by the time he stands up and shuffles away crying.

It doesn't take a rocket scientist to put two-and-two together and see they pushed the kid.

I bite down on my lip to keep a lid on my do-good sensor. Doing good ain't the point of us skipping school. And it sure ain't the type of morals I was raised with.

Sylvia's giggles at the chubby geek kid's misery and rough chokes on the blunt bring me back from the moral tango my *brain danced. Fuck wrong or right, I thought, snatching the blunt from her hands.*

"Puff and pass girl," I warn before pulling real hard on the bud. "That's a cardinal rule when in space."

"Space?"

"Space," I emphasize with flailed hands to highlight my point. "You know, getting high into the clouds with this joint shit."

"Ohhhhh..." She said before falling into yet, another fit of giggles. Frankly, I was getting real sick of her. "Smoking weed!"

Sylvia continues to babble on about being able to see if the sky really is blue as my mind drifts into the ether. I wonder where that kid went and what the hell his name is. Those dudes who knocked him down the hill like Friday night's trash looked really familiar too, in fact, like I'd smoked with them before. That do-good sensor kicks off in my head even after I finish the blunt. I didn't adore the heaviness in my chest at the reality that we'd stood by and laughed while he got kicked. That he was falling down in misery while we got high in the sky.

Then I hear the cries.

Those same whimpers from before are not loud and ringing in my ears. It's Geeky Kid. The increased volume of his cries let me know he's right beside me now, yet I don't see anyone when I open my eyes to scan the empty schoolyard.

"So you kickin it with snow bunnies now or what?"

The coarse voice jerked me from my thoughts and I blinked hard to focus on the set of three new faces before me.

"What do you guys think happens when black and white mix together?" I hear Sylvia ask innocently to the guys ahead.

They laugh of course.

"Why don't you and Dev answer us that?"

It isn't really a question. More so, it's a dare. A challenge to both she and I, but I can't think straight with all the crying in my ears from the kid I no longer saw.

"Yo Sylvia chill on that black and white shit." I grumble at her.

"Barbie is high as hell!" One of the dudes chortle.

"Wake up and stop being a fake bitch, Devin. Can't you see me talking to you?" The one in the middle demands.

Then the crying stops. And the fog clears enough for me to identify the all black american teens glaring daggers at me.

"Ty?" I ask.

"So now you see me. Smell the coffee and look at me when I talk to you. You murderer."

"Say what?"

"You're there. And I'm here. Because of YOU!"

Ty raises his hand to punch the living shit out of me, and it's a blow I merely don't got the energy to block. That blow, like that stupid do-good meter, was gonna hit me full frontal and without a means to dodge.

Suddenly there's yelling in the background.

Not the background, I realized, but far off into the distance there's a girl pacing backwards from us and calling out to me. It's Sylvia.

"Black and white?!" She screams, her blond hair whipping as carefree in the wind as her continued laughter. "You get gray!"

I woke up to the sound of the car engine stopping, I looked out the window to see that we had made it home. That must have been a dream, I thought. A nightmare. I knew if Ty was still alive, he wouldn't dis me that way. I remember Tyrone having strong views of things, but it was never a cigarette or something couldn't fix. He was a dumb guy, but not a racist. I shook it off and made it inside. I remembered Patrice wanting me to deliver her message to Yvonne. I might as well get it over with before I forget, I thought. When I walked inside I called her name throughout the house, but there was silence. "Yvonne, where you at?" Again, I got the same response. I looked in the basement, she wasn't there. That was when I began to worry. All the memories of Michael came to me, and I grew frantic. "Has anybody seen Yvonne?" Everyone shook their heads and started calling her name as I did. Did she run away? Was she murdered? Stolen?

And that was when the phone rang.

I ran for it and answered. "Is this the residence of Timothy Blake?" A male voice asked. A cold voice. A sad voice "Well, sir we wanted to inform you that, uh, Helen

Cooper passed away last night. She suffered a cardiac arrest, and no one could save her. I'm very sorry..." He hung up, and I was panting, and worried and sad and mad, and angry. I dashed out of the house, desperate to find my little sister. I sprinted for the backyard and saw the shed. Please God, let my sister be okay. I prayed. That's all I thought about. My little piece of sanity was MIA, and I was going insane. This was not how I pictured my birthday to turn out even if I remembered it. I ripped the shed door open, nearly off its hinges, and gasped at what I saw: Helen and a guy nakedly and sweatily grinding on each other in front of me...making out...in front of me...undressed...in front of me. Except, it wasn't Helen this time...it was Yvonne Elizabeth Masters. My Yvonne. With a guy. *Naked!* In the shed. Alone. Together. Doing things twelve-year-olds shouldn't.

And just like that ...I saw my life slip away...I saw it flash...in front of me, also. I hit the ground, and after that was darkness.

Seventeen

SET IN STONE

I DREADED SEEING THAT place again. The hospital. The white, sad, room. I woke up to see the face of a nurse adjusting my bed, giving me extra pillows, and such.

"Where am I?" My voice was groggy, and dry when I asked.

The nurse was quick to assuage my doubts. "Oh, don't worry sweetheart. You're in a good place. This is the hospital."

I nodded. Sadly, that didn't do any justice for me. I was still overwhelmed with sadness. I couldn't— didn't want to— face the fact that Yvonne was no longer my little girl. She was some monster that I just couldn't save. I had to face that Yvonne had some of that Cooper blood running through her veins. And I was no healer, I couldn't just change genetics.

However, what I could change though, was my environment. I thought about for a long time and decided not to punish myself for what I did. The arson. I had every intention on burning that damn house to the ground, it was closure. Just because I had no family left...didn't mean I had to kill myself over it. It was inevitable, right? To lose everyone you had...I guess I deserved it. All the sin I committed...I guess it was just meant for me. I had to face the fact that I had no one, and no one wanted me. No one wanted this nobody. Especially when this loner needed somebody at that moment, more than ever in his life.

The doctor came in and smiled at me. Behind him was Pastor Tim and the same social worker from before.

"Hello sleepyhead." The doctor said to me.

He looked like a cool guy.

"What?" I mumbled. I felt like I was high. "Why do I feel so stoned?" I slurred.

Did I just say that? Was that my voice?

The doctor laughed. "Yeah, the IV can do that to you. Don't worry though, it's only a little dose of sodium chloride. It'll wear off soon." He studied everything carefully, with a pondering frown. "All right Devin—your vitals seem to be normal. Nothing to worry about so far."

"So far?" I asked. "Huh?"

"Well, you had a severe anxiety attack. It wasn't the worst I'd seen, so you should be fine. However, I will be prescribing some pills for you. I was just suggesting that you seek help. Therapy is what I mean."

I glared at him as if he spat in my face. "I'm not crazy! There's no way—"

"To get better, Mr. Cooper. You are very much suffering from depression and I just want to give you something to take the *edge* off. Your foster dad told me all about the stress you were going through. This will help you."

I turned away.

This was what I hated. Speaking and having no one listen. That was just frustrating. I had to calm down though. This crap in my veins was making me calm anyway. No matter how much I wanted to feel different, I couldn't.

"I'll catch you later Devin. I just need to get these prescriptions to the nurse, and if all your vitals are well you can leave soon." He exited the room swiftly.

There was just the three of us left. If I had the strength to go, I would've, in that moment. Pastor Tim came up to me and smiled his warm, oblivious, "I'll never hurt you" smile. He never did anything to harm me; of course, I just couldn't look him in the eye.

"Well, the police are still investigating who burned your old house down. It might take them a while, but they'll get to the culprit in no time. I assure you this." His face was set in stone as he said it, a mask of solemnity.

It didn't frighten me, because I knew that if they did catch me, they'd never be able to rebuild those memories. The house may be standing once again, but my life would never be connected to it anymore. I knew where my heart was, and it sure wasn't here...in DC. The first chance that would come by me, I'd be bound to the place I experienced at least a semblance of normalcy— or, Queens New York.

Pastor Tim shook his head and whispered, "This kind of ruined your birthday surprise from us all."

"Huh?" I looked at him in confusion.

I hadn't known that people actually cared about that. Most would just look at me and say: *so you survived another year, huh?* Well, Helen would say that...every year. I guess I just wasn't used to a normal "Happy Birthday!" much less a "surprise."

"Yeah, we just got you a little something to remember us by. It's outside, I drove it here— to the hospital."

I gulped, and closed my eyes. This was not happening. How in the hell would I pay him back now? "If you're saying what I think you're saying...please pinch me."

"Yup! I, uh, made some calls here and there, and— bam!" He slapped his hands together. I jumped. "Your car is as good as new. I took it out of the shop, and I fixed it up— now it's my gift to you, how 'bout it?" I chuckled at that frequently used saying of his.

He continued, "The family has something else for you back at the house. I just need to know when you'll be released." And then his face went solemn again. That mask of imperfection. "I heard about Ms. Cooper? Uh ...your mom...I mean, the social worker called and told me all about it a few hours ago. And I just thought I should come in and cheer you up with..." He looked down for a long time, until when finally he came up and said very sadly, "I know what it's like to lose your mom, and it really hurts, so...if you need someone to relate to then...you've got someone. I understand."

I looked at him for longer than I intended to. It was ironic, I guess Yvonne was wrong, he really could understand. Talk about ignorance. As much as I wanted to sit there and bag on my sister, I knew I couldn't just sit there and blame her for stuff. I've been trying so hard to get her to do the right thing, while I realized that it wasn't my job to do those things. It was Helen's, as well as it was Quincy's. I just had to understand that I was her brother, and not her parent. But what other parent would she have, besides me? I was all she had, and she was all I had, we were supposed to have each others' backs. I couldn't deny the sense betrayal I felt, I had understood that Yvonne was growing up— but at twelve? She's still a baby...was supposed to be a pure child. I couldn't just privilege her all her life. Although my new outlook made no sense to me, I had to accept it. I had to build my own sanity this time.

I snapped out of my funk and uttered, "You mentioned something about 'remembering you by'. What was that about?"

I really needed to know that. I wanted to move away from them, but at the same time I had no place else to go.

"Oh, that." He began to mentally kick himself.

Like he thought I would forget about that.

"Actually, Mr. Cooper," Ms. Prowl interjected. I had forgotten she was in the room. I remembered speaking with her three months ago. She was prettier than the last time I saw her. Last time, she looked older— dry. Mean. "There is a family member who wants to claim Yvonne and you." She opened her briefcase and pulled out a folder. She opened it and read out loud, "A Mr. and Mrs. Carlson, in Richmond, Virginia. They claim to be your grandparents. Do you know them?" I was looking at her in disbelief by then. Someone wanted us? We had family left? Someone was there? I wasn't alone? Whoever these people were, I wanted to thank them and cry.

"N-No. Is there a reason they decided to speak up now? After all we've been through?" Ms. Prowl began digging in her files again, but this time she pulled out a folded piece of paper.

"They thought you'd ask that, so here's their number. Call them as soon as you get the chance." She looked at the Pastor who was smiling at me the whole time.

I looked up at him from my bed, and said tiredly, "Thank you for all you've done, sir. Is there a way I could repay you?" Even a thousand thank you's couldn't match the kindness he'd shown me. I didn't even know if I was worthy to say thank you to him.

"Yes. Live the longest and happiest life you can. Be happy— I wish you both well in Virginia."

"Aw, shucks— come here!" I sat, opened my arms, and gave him a hug. I pulled at my IV, and backed up. That stuff was tugging at my veins, I didn't mess with that.

When we parted, he looked me in the eyes and said, "Well, I'll let you rest awhile. Oh, here—" he dug into his pockets and handed me his cell phone. "Give 'em a call. Get to know 'em. I'll be in the waiting room. Let's go Lisa!"

They left, and I fiddled with the number for some time. I had to swallow my pride this time. I dialed the number, and waited as I listened to the dial tone.

Goodness, it felt like forever until I heard a calm, southern male voice at the other end.

"Carlson residence." I was choking. I felt like I had swallowed a dinosaur egg. I just couldn't find my voice. "Is somebody there? Dan, if that's you—"

"It's Devin Cooper!" I blurted. I cupped my hand over my mouth after I did that. I wanted to clobber myself with a hammer. That was dumb! *Good going Devin!*

"D-Devin? Hold on son...Hattie! Eddie's boy is on the telephone!"

"Eddie's boy?" I heard a distant voice exclaim. "Hello? Oh, what was the name...Damon? Hello Damon, this is your grandmamma Hattie, but everyone calls me Mamma Dean."

"Hi...Mamma Dean. I'm Devin Coo—"

"Cooper! I know son! You think I wouldn't know my own grandson?"

Maybe, I thought.

"I done heard about your Mamma. I am so sorry 'bout what happened. I done heard about you on the television. All this time I was workin' on a way to get on down there and get you, but my diabetes been actin' up and I couldn't travel. I'm sorry baby. No one knew how to get to you!"

I nodded, and nosedived into a question, "So how'd you get to me now?" I was preparing for the disappointment.

"Well, somebody called here and asked for Eddie, I told him he was out at the moment, and he told me instead that he had the number to the prison in Washington DC that I have to call— 'cause I ain't know your Mamma was in the big house then. So when I called, they done told me about your Mamma. They asked about relation and I told them that I was lookin' for you! I am so glad that you called. I just hope...ne'er mind." She paused. She seemed pensive.

"What? You okay?" I asked.

This conversation was overwhelming. "I hope you don't hate me. Or Edward— your father for not being there. Your Mamma ain't want nothing to do with us."

"Why would you think that? I...strongly disliked Hel—my mother. She wanted nothing good for me. I just don't know why."

"Yeah, well thank God he called us. 'Cause now you'll be safe." She said that with determination. "Whoever that man was, he called at this number. What a nice man. He said that he was a friend of Eddie's. But I never known Eddie to have any white friends. No offense." My mind was reeling. I didn't know how to react. I guess it was the IV, because I felt suddenly lightheaded again. Just as I had before I passed out. So Pastor Tim had investigated and more than pulled some strings. He had found my family. I guess he knew I just wasn't happy at his house...not truly happy. I felt hot tears slip down my cheeks. I guess they just snuck up on me. That was too much, I didn't know he could make miracles happen.

"Are you still there, baby? Oh, dang it— Eddie just walked through the door. Eddie guess who on the phone? Here, it'll surprise you." I swallowed hard. I didn't know if I could do this. I thought I was strong... that I could do anything I was tough enough to do. But talking to this man would be a life altering moment.

"Who is this?" A raspy voice asked. He sounded kind of like myself.

"This is Devin."

"Devin, my son, Devin? You're my son, kid. Helen decided to let me see you?" I guess he didn't know about her yet.

"Um, something like that. You are Edward Carlson, right?"

"Yes." He spoke slowly.

"Did you know I had a sister?" I said, for some reason. I heard him gasp over the phone. "Her name's Yvonne."

"I didn't know she had another kid. What else don't I know...son?"

I had yearned to hear those words all those years. Even the times I lived with Quincy, I wanted to know Eddie. All this time...this was what I needed. My father.

"There's a whole lot, Pops. A whole lot."

And for some reason, I had remembered the time Tyrone mooned the dorks on the school bus and ran.

He was being a real ass.

EPILOGUE: 1 year later

"Yo, man, pass me the ball!" Bone commanded in a fierce huff while blocking me on the court. It was a hot AF day in Richmond and we were playing basketball at my homeboy's house since he had the biggest back-yard. Well, Mamma Dean's back yard was large, but always filled with farm equipment and field workers. It had been a whole year since making the move to normalcy from the hellhole that was DC. There was so much that transpired in such a short time, including me getting some friends, excelling in high school, and actually taking pride in my grades and giving a fuck about my future.

I shoved the taller, ghostly skinny guy aside to make a grab for the basketball from Zay.

We were split into two teams with Malik, another tall black teen but with skin like onyx, and me. Zay and Bone were on the other team.

Zay, while slightly shorter than my six foot four frame, artfully dodged my grab, swirled around, and dunked the ball.

I glared at his skinny body hanging from the basket. "All right, all right, we get it. Y'all won."

Bone ran up to catch Zay as he fell from the basket. They danced in that weird half-cradle half hug position and chanted "We da best!" over and over.

"Fuck y'all, man!" Malik barked beside me. "Y'all fucking cheated anyway."

"Nah!" Zay laughed once on solid ground. "We da best. We won. Fair and square."

"You ain't mad, are you?" Bone drawled in that deeply southern accent of his. "Because I'll fix you a bottle if all you gonna do is cry!"

Malik charged for him, but I held him back.

"Chill out," I told them. "We gonna do a rematch."

Zay's laughs stopped at my words. "A rematch? So y'all tryna lose more money?"

A tic started in my jaw at the stakes. We often did this. For whatever reason, we often gambled money, weed, or various other favors or farmwork over basketball games. I know how it sounded, but there was so little to do here besides eat and play ball, and we all worked for Mamma Dean for minimum wage on the farm so we sometimes traded duties over games. For instance, I hated mowing the lawn, as it was something I never had to get accustomed to in DC, where we never had grass, so I gambled that chore with Zay, who loved it but hated shoveling hay. So we switched.

I groaned as I recalled the stakes of this game, though, before responding to Zay.

"We ain't gonna lose." I stated evenly, not letting on how nervous I was to potentially lose another game.

"Oh, really?" Bone mocked, turning serious. "Well, if that's the case, then let's up the ante."

Malik, who always took life way too seriously, straightened. "What's up, pussy?"

Bone chuckled at Malik's fury before saying, "Double or nothing. What y'all think?"

"We got this. We game, right DC?" Malik asked me. I was nicknamed DC for several obvious reasons after we met. DC stood for the place from which I was raised as well as my newly adopted initials: Devin Carlson.

I extended my fist to Malik where we pounded on it. "Game. Let's do this."

"Cool." Bone agreed, bouncing the ball idly. "But let's break for ten. I need some air. This heat is killing me."

Malik scoffed. "Aww, is the little baby sweaty and tired? Or you just scared to get your ass whipped for real this time?"

Bone and Malik charged each other, and while Malik was shorter he weighed much more than the rail thin guy we nicknamed Bone for his ghostly appearance. I rolled my eyes and pivoted out of the way of the fight. They were only wrestling, nothing serious, but it got tiring wrangling these dudes in. I allowed their voices to drift into background noise as I recalled the past, of the former perpetual restlessness I felt from fighting life all the time in DC.

Shaking those memories away, I went dutifully in search of a much needed refreshment inside the small house. The house could almost be referred to as what they call "farmhouse" style, had it not been for the outdated paint job and fucked up shingle panneling on the outside. There was nothing wrong with it, nothing at all, and being as I lived on the streets at one point when Vonnie and I lived in New York I was no one to judge. After Quincy died, we lived with my uncle Troy, his wife and two kids, Jerome and Georgia, for a short time in Jersey before we were forced to move back to Helen's before the start of my sophomore year. While we lived mostly as fugitives, I wouldn't trade my time away from Hellhole Helen for anything.

"Come to papa..." I sang before placing the entire bottle of Tropicana orange juice to my lips. The cool liquid provided instant relief from the scorching Richmond heat. Sweat pooled down my naked back and I all but groaned as the contents of the bottle nearly emptied.

"Hey!" A shrill female voice touched my ears.

I flinched from the unexpected presence and caginess of the unseen woman. I didn't need to turn around from the fridge to know who she was, however. I knew that voice anywhere.

"What did I tell you boys about drinking straight from my orange juice bottles?" Shayne, Zay's older sister and guardian, barked from behind me as she entered the room.

"Yo!" I protested when she marched over to snatch the half empty bottle from my grasp. "I was almost finished though."

She crossed her arms irritatedly across her chest, glaring up at me. "You gonna pay for that?"

A tic worked its way in my jaw. I was accustomed to her usual bitchiness, as she worked long hours as a nurse in the city and often sported bags under her pretty brown eyes. I understood the origin of her fury and disappointment at watching me guzzle her only bottle of juice, but damn it if I wasn't thirsty as hell after that game. Zay bought his A-game today and I wasn't about to be bested by that sports newbie when I'd been playing ball for years.

I returned her glare. "You want me to pay for that, for real?"

"Hell yeah!" She bellowed, and it was only now when I noticed what she was wearing.

I licked my lips as I studied her luscious curves in her silk nightgown. I scanned my way up and down the length of her short frame, stopping to appreciate the effect of my eyes on her body. Her nipples pebbled under the intensity of my stare and I had to cuss myself to keep from reaching out and tasting her.

"How much I owe you, Shay?" I husked, my eyes still focused on her nipples.

She retreated, her breathing coming uneven in pitch. "U-Um, stop playing, D. You know how much it is…"

I followed her, stalked her, into the corner of the small kitchen until I heard her ass bump into the sink.

She placed hands on my chest and cut her eyes beyond me. "D, for real, what if the guys see us?"

"How much." I rasped, pressing my sweaty chest into her silk-clad one. "Do you want?"

A brief hint of indecision flashed in her eyes before she pulled my lips to hers. The kiss heated me in other ways on this scorching hot day, and even though I knew we were risking it, I couldn't help but lift her into my arms. She wrapped her chubby legs around my waist and I carried her down the hall without ever breaking the kiss we craved. I needed her. Right now. I had never needed to be inside a woman so damn bad it felt like my heart would stop if I didn't get her to the frilly outfitted queen bed in time.

"God, I've missed you." She moaned from under me as I slid her nightgown off.

I kissed a trail from her belly to her lips before responding to her. "I missed you, too. You the one that always gotta *go to work* and all..."

She giggled and my dick jerked at the sound. "So sorry I've got to make a living around here. Too bad this rent doesn't pay itself."

"I know." I agreed playfully between more kisses. "You know I can't get enough of you, girl..."

After a few minutes of passionate fucking, we collapsed onto the bed. Her snores permeated the air and I wrapped my arms around her, needing her closeness all of a sudden.

I lay in bed reflecting on how my life came to be in Virginia. Of all the hardships Vonnie and I faced after all the running. Always running to find a home and never having one. Life on the farm was hard work, and there were days it felt like I'd die from laboring out in all that heat, but for the first time in my life I made an honest wage in a house where I was respected. My father, Eddie, existed more like my fourth homie, as he lived in a cabin on Mamma Dean's land and came to work the farm and visit me every chance he got.

"I admit." He told me the day I moved down here. "I ain't the fathering type. But you'll never need for anything so long as you let me be there. That goes for both of you."

We dapped on it, and have been tight ever since. I understood it wasn't the average father-son relationship, but what I valued the most about our bond was that it was honest. I always felt like a burden to Quincy, who barely saw me as a human being. In all honesty, if I wasn't running drugs for him or making his life profitable in some way, then he would have sent me packing ages ago. After Mikey was killed, I saw a different side of him, though. He was edgier, and made crazier moves in the streets when it came to dealing. I didn't care if his moves bought him more danger to be honest, but I couldn't tolerate it bringing any harm to Vonnie.

Yvonne, I thought. My heart filled with pride at the thought of my new sister. She had since come *way* out of her shell since last year, and it felt like I never truly saw her. Never saw her for the woman she was becoming after all that time. Since we were adopted by the Carlsons, her eyes never took on that far away look they'd get in DC. While no replacement, I tried being the best brother to keep her sane. To keep her here with me mentally and physically after all the tragedy we'd experienced. Her grades improved in school, too, since moving to Richmond, but she still lacked in the friend department. In all honesty, it concerned me to see her never bring any friends around.

A pretty smile cut through my memories just then, making my heart race with longing.

Patrice Newbern.

Last I heard before moving away, she'd given birth to her baby and took off to Wisconsin. Why Wisconsin? I'm not too sure, since I'd never heard of any black people just living it up in the cheese capital. If my theory was right, I wondered, then she'd have one of two reasons for being there: college or a guy. But not just any guy. Kale McAllen, one of my former...friends, one could call it, made me a promise when I left for New York a few years ago. A promise to keep her safe if anything happened while I was away. He'd admitted that he was in love with her one day, and I always wondered what happened to him since leaving DC. Maybe Kale was in Wisconsin. Maybe he was able to get her to love him back. He and I had a dark, shared past, one I didn't dare dredge up for fear of collapsing and caving into the darkness.

I hated the way my chest squeezed at the thought of Trice out there, a single mom and facing life alone. I wished, in that moment, that it was her in my arms instead. Her I was kissing in intimate places, and her who snored peacefully beneath me.

"Dev?" A meek voice asked.

I looked down to meet Shay's large brown eyes in the shadows. "Yes, baby?"

A brief silence ensued before she whispered. "You love me, right?"

"What?" I asked, totally thrown off guard by her words.

She giggled and hugged me tighter. "You heard me, DC. Do you love me? Can you see yourself with me?"

"But Zay..." I start.

"Zay, is getting older." She supplied. "And I need to start living for myself. I'm not getting any younger– I'm twenty-one for god's sake. And I was thinking that maybe after you graduate, then–"

"I'm enlisting!" I blurt, needing her words to stop so that the ache in my chest would ease.

She sat up. "You're what?!"

I nodded, groaning a little from it all. "Yeah...I haven't told anyone yet, so...just keep it under wraps for now. Okay?"

"Dev," she whispered, her tone tortured. "Why would you do this? Don't you like it here? Why are you trying to leave me...?"

"I–" I opened my mouth to tell her I'd never leave her, that I loved her, too, when a shrill scream broke out in the distance that made me eat those words. A scream. I knew that voice. I knew it all too well, and I'm suddenly back in Helen's house running through the halls to get to my little sister. Readying myself to fight whatever monster was hurting her from within the shadows.

Except, this isn't Helen's house. It's Zay and Shay's, and I'm running like a half naked mad man to the backyard where my sister's screams are emanating.

"Vonnie!" I scream as I burst through the kitchen door into the yard. Everyone pauses when they get a look at my frantic face. My eyes are probably red as they scan through the crowd to find her familiar face.

I race to her and sweep her into my arms. "Are you okay?"

She wriggles out of my arms. "Dev, ew, you're all sweaty and naked. Gross!"

"How did you get here?" I asked, still not sold on her welfare.

She rolled her eyes. "Mr. Eddie gave me a ride since he had an errand to run in town. Calm down, I'm okay."

"What are you doing here, Von?" I ask.

She glances at the crowd, and I'm immediately reminded of the homies behind me.

Zay steps up. "Hey, DC, Von came to play some ball. That's all. She was whipping our asses while you was in there fucking Shay."

My cheeks flame as the guys begin to hoot and holler teasing obscenities. I gulp and glare at him. "Zay, really man? You ain't have to say all that in front of Vonnie like that."

He frowned. "Why? Ain't it true though?"

"Hell yeah!" Bone corroborated behind me. "She ain't no baby, she'll be all right. Plus, she played your team while you were in there smashing."

"And what happened?" Malik teased him. "Come on, tell the man."

Bone rolled his eyes and crossed his arms over his chest. "Y'all won."

Malik fell out laughing at his words. "Come on, one more time for the one time! Who won?"

"Y'all." Bone grumbled.

"Who da best?" Malik taunted, doing the running-man.

Zay spoke up. "Vonnie won y'all the game. So, congratulations."

Vonnie joined Malik in dancing as I listened to Zay. "I guess y'all win the bet, too."

"Really?" I asked, incredulous.

"Yep." Zay agreed while digging in his pockets. He looked around before handing me the small black box. "You won it. Fair and square."

I nodded, licking my suddenly dry lips at the mention of the private item we wagered on this basketball game. I opened it to see the thing I originally asked him for a loan to buy before he told me of the piece of jewelry that belonged to their family. This item was passed down from generation to generation, and I insisted on buying it from him, like an honest man, but he only laughed and said to wager it from him if I wanted it.

Well, I wagered. Or, rather, Vonnie unknowingly did on my behalf, and won. Won the item I'd intended on presenting to Shayne, my girl, once I turned eighteen.

A ring.

So much of my life lived perfectly in between sanity and dysfunction, and that gray area made up for the monsters that created me. However, I knew this one thing to be real:

Nothing would ever be the same after this.

Author's Note

HOPE YOU ENJOYED THE BOOK! Thank you for reading GRAY, my very first novel written at fifteen years old. As a token of my gratitude, here's an excerpt to *LIGHT,* the second book in the *REAL* SERIES

LIGHT

"WHAT'S THAT?" GABBY ASKED me in Spanish when she walked into my room unannounced, eyeing down the eyesore of a poster. It was the beautiful image of Emilio Ricotti and me hugging each other, but his head was barbarically hacked away from the picture. Emilio and I were always breaking up and making up on a regular basis- I was the usual one to make it clear that we weren't speaking or together. Gabriella Reyes was my mother, and she knew very little English. After all, we moved from Spanish-speaking Florida only three years ago, so she was a little star crossed between a hot dog and a futon. But I loved her anyway.

I learned most of my English through school. I was listening to music on my iPod, and she sort of scared me.

"¡Dios mío!" I exclaimed, placing a hand to my heart as I stood and walked over to her. "Ma! Knock next time." I imitated knocking gestures with my hands. *"Knock!"*

I was determined for her to understand English. I ushered Gabby out the door and shut it. She was so annoying! Barging into my room without knocking should be a sin. She was very religious so I knew that would have made her emphasize her entrance. Whatever it was she needed to tell me so badly...never mind. I threw my iPod in my drawer and cut the TV on. There was nothing on but a bunch of paid programming and cooking shows. I wasn't that much into infomercials and frying eggs, so I switched it off. Shying from that, I guess it was all right to mention my twenty-four year old brother who was still mooching off my parents. He had a room down the hall from mine, which he used to sneak *gringas* upstairs. I was the only one who knew about them, he didn't know I knew, but I wasn't going to let him know that. His name is Enrique Reyes; a playful post grad that said he would join the army once he "got on his feet." I didn't believe it until I saw it in writing. Which I still didn't.

I actually knew what Gabriella waltzed in my room for. I think we all could guess why. She didn't trust me after that...incident eighteen months ago. However, I assured her that I was no longer a dumb girl. What happened was the past and I was willing to get over it. I had no idea if my dad, Pablo would get over it. Well, he was stern and alpha male, so I doubted he'd be showing his emotions soon.

Pablo Reyes worked dayshift and night shift in retail. We had a family business sort of thing going on. My dad bought and sold property in El Salvador, but in the U.S., he just brought buildings and turned them into stores. Like tattoo bars, Deli's, convenient stores, and Laundromats. It was a bit more fun to just walk in the store and ask the employees to make you a sandwich on the spot. I know they just put it on my dad's tab though. When Pablo came home the house would always seem to light up. We're laughing and joking or dancing or singing just for kicks. His face lights up when he comes in to see us all there— alive and well.

I got up from bed, threw my shoes on, and combed my shoulder length ringlets out. I sprayed it with some oil sheen and threw my hat on. Next week would be the first week of my junior year in high school. I could not wait to leave school after senior year though, and to me it was the beginning of the end. After school, I'll probably find an apartment somewhere, not here in Queens though. There was no way.

When I walked through the living room to leave, I was feeling for change in my pocket. Yes, there was a twenty in there. I was wearing my mini skirt and was surprised that I found anything in there at all. I rarely put items in that tiny little pocket. I shrugged and exited the house without waking anyone up. I guess I was always a morning person, not many people would enjoy waking up and walking to the store for something. Anything, really.

I went to *Reyes,* our family store, and saw someone I thought I'd never see again. I truly thought he'd run away this time. Ironic that he was in the same store the same time as me. I could feel the hate bubble inside me as I walked toward the minors' section to buy my item.

"What's happening Ray—"

I got what I needed and dashed for the check-out. He followed me.

I handed the cashier the money and then exploded, "Juan, leave me alone!" He was on my trail as I attempted to get away. I stopped and waited for him to walk up to me.

"I just want—"

I swung my loaded shopping bag in his face.

It threw him back for a minute, but gave me just enough time to make it down Elmer Street.

"I just want to see her..." was his voice trailing off from the distance.

Once I made it inside the house, I shut the door and locked it. He knew where I lived of course, and I didn't want to see the bastard. I looked down to see a crying little girl crawl toward me and touch my toes. I sat my bag of pampers down on the floor, and picked her up. She stopped crying when I held her. Her eyes were glistening and she was pouting.

"You're ugly when you cry Jasmine. " She smiled, not understanding a word I was saying. I guess I never got around to mentioning that I was a mom.

About the Author

Since the age of twelve, Laura could always be found writing. She writes within a wide array of genres, including paranormal, drama, slice of life, and (her favorite) romance. In her free time, if she's not writing, she's reading or listening to a steamy audio-book. Her most notable works include Something About Kyle and her ongoing, The REAL Series, which explores the narratives of various, interconnected young adults.

As an author, Laura aims to push boundaries and leave a lasting impact on her community. Her journey taught her the importance of perseverance, creativity, and staying true to one's unique vision. Support her craft by purchasing from her bookstore.